The two lines of verse quoted on p. 127 are from 'Cairngorm, November 1971' by Martyn Berry in *Poems of the Scottish Hills*, Aberdeen University Press, and are reprinted by permission of the author.

I've travelled the world twice over,
Met the famous: saints and sinners,
Poets and artists, kings and queens,
Old stars and hopeful beginners,
I've been where no-one's been before,
Learned secrets from writers and cooks
All with one library ticket
To the wonderful world of books.

© JANICE JAMES.

THE HILLS ARE LONELY

Gavin McKendrick had brought his thirteen-year-old daughter, Kate, to a remote cottage in the Scottish Highlands to escape the constant reminders of his wife, killed in an accident. Kate roamed the moors and along the shores of the loch, her heart heavy. Only her form mistress, Sheina McDonald, was aware of her unhappiness and longed to help her. It was the wild cat that was to change their lives — alone and free, and beautiful, he won Kate's heart.

Books by Joyce Stranger
in the Ulverscroft Large Print Series:

REX
CASEY

JOYCE STRANGER

THE HILLS ARE LONELY

Complete and Unabridged

ULVERSCROFT
Leicester

First published in Great Britain in 1993 by
Souvenir Press Limited
London

First Large Print Edition
published June 1994
by arrangement with
Souvenir Press Limited
London

British Library CIP Data

Stranger, Joyce
    The hills are lonely.—Large print ed.—
Ulverscroft large print series: general fiction
I. Title
823.914 [F]

ISBN 0–7089–3099–9

Published by
F. A. Thorpe (Publishing) Ltd.
Anstey, Leicestershire

Set by Words & Graphics Ltd.
Anstey, Leicestershire
Printed and bound in Great Britain by
T. J. Press (Padstow) Ltd., Padstow, Cornwall

This book is printed on acid-free paper

1

HIGH on the hill the wind savaged the trees. The animals hated the wind. The invisible monster that tore out of the sky, shrieking at them. The fierce unseen mouth that screamed among the trees. Banshee noises in the undergrowth. Ghosts and demons flicking at fur and driving the blinding rain into their unprotected eyes.

The cat was lonely. He was a young cat, just over seven months old, and his mother had been killed by a rock fall. He had been her only kit in what was to be her last litter. The father was a true wild cat, fierce and predatory, hunting high among the rocks, coming to her briefly, and leaving her again.

The little animal was not fully grown. Though not a pure wild cat, he had never known man. His mother had belonged to an old lady who died when the cat was only ten months old. She had fled from the suddenly bustling cottage, from

1

the coroner, the police, the inquisitive villagers.

Old Martha Cameron had no relatives. She had outlived them all. She died of a heart attack, one bright May evening when the moon shone full. Nobody knew she had a cat. Few knew anything about her. She died as she lived, alone and uncomplaining.

The old lady had been proud, independent, refusing help from them, although she was over eighty. Now they wondered if they could have done more for her, could have penetrated her isolation, could have made her life easier.

The man who cleared up the old lady's property marvelled at the little she possessed. He did not realise that she had a cat, even though he saw the empty saucers on the floor. He picked them up and packed them with the rest of her goods. Martha did not believe in tinned food and there were no betraying labels to reveal that here was an animal that had been petted and housed.

Little grey Heyda hid herself. She

learned to live alone, to rely on her own hunting ability, and by the time she was ten years old had mothered many kittens. The keepers hated her and her young. They waged constant war, but Heyda was cunning.

The young cat mourned for his mother. She had died before he was fully independent. There were no other wild cats for miles around. The beasts on the hill hated him. Hare and rabbit, and all the little birds gave their warning calls when he came.

Cat. Cat. Cat.

The sounds echoed long after he had passed. Shriek from every beak, as bright eyes spied the ripple in the grass. The thump on the ground of the watching sentry in the warren, as the wind brought news of his coming. The fleeing hare that outran him every time. They all feared him. He was terror, stalking on four padded paws, moving softly, death unseen until that last fatal pounce.

He was driven to raiding the hen runs and the duck ponds, and the farmers were always watching for him, guns loaded. The gamekeepers hated him too as wild cats took the grouse chicks. All were sure he was a true wild cat.

There was no sanctuary, anywhere on the hill. Enemies surrounded him. Winter tormented him. He was always hungry and he feared the noisy invisible wind that so often battered the moors.

He crouched in a tiny cave, hollowed out in the rock and lined with dead leaves. It was away from the wind, but the wind still haunted him. It rustled the dead leaves so that they sounded like the pitter of tiny paws. It cracked a branch from a nearby tree with the sound of gunshot and he huddled against the ground, making himself small, fearing that there would be footsteps to follow.

Fear. He knew fear too well. Knew the panic as a giant stalked him, gun aimed, and he ran for his life. Knew panic as the wind churned the wet grasses, searching into his lair, chilling him through his thick fur.

He was a handsome beast, and would be a King of Cats when grown. Black stripes tiger-marked the thick grey fur, inheritance from his father. He crouched, his dense tail wound round his body to

4

give him extra warmth. He lay with fore-paws curled, claws sheathed, the moon lighting the white patch on his chest and the white round his muzzle.

Fear shadowed his green eyes, black rimmed, the pupils a slit in the darkness, as he watched the moon slide up the sky, playing tag with the racing clouds. Prick ears moved to and fro as he listened. The untidy half-moon was reflected deep in his glowing eyes.

He listened to the savage March wind that howled defiance at the night. Listened to the trees that shrieked as they bent almost to the ground. Listened to the birds that cried in fear as nests were blown down, and their sheltering branches torn from parent trunks and little boulders crashed and rumbled as they moved on the slope.

He was hungry, but he dared not venture out into the wildness. He licked at a puddle on the ground, disliking the sharp metallic taste of the rock beneath it, but he needed to drink.

He moaned to himself softly and fluffed his fur. He was cold and rain now teased out of clouds that gathered ever more darkly and hid the moon. He lay, whiskers twitching, and longed for the endless night to give way to dawn, for the wind to drop and the rain to cease.

He planned, in the morning, to slip down the mountainside. He preferred night, but this year the high winds had come with dusk, had savaged ever more strongly, and he could either hunt by day or stay hungry.

There were hens loose in the cottage on the hill. Yet another old woman lived there now, and she did not seem to notice the raiding cat. Sometimes she put food down: rabbit legs which he carried up to his lair above her home. The thought of them brought saliva to his mouth and he licked his lips. He was unaware that she thought she was feeding her own cat, a placid domestic tabby, now slow and old, who was suffering from his theft of her meals.

There was no threat from the old lady who remained unaware of her frequent visitor or that her own pet was often hungry.

The farm below the cottage was not

safe. It housed two Jack Russell terriers which were borrowed by everyone because of their prowess with rats. The young cat had seen them challenge a vixen, had watched her fight them, and creep away, bleeding from a dozen bites. He had heard her soft whimpers of pain as she licked her wounds.

He had seen her grow thin, unable to walk on a festering leg. Had known when she died. The birds and the beasts all yelled when she came, too, but as she grew slower and lay watching death approach her, their cries had ceased. She no longer threatened them.

He needed a mate. He longed for another cat for company and to fill a devouring need that he could not identify. He asked the wind daily for news, but it brought nothing but the smell of hens and geese and ducks. He needed company. Another body to lie against, to lick in companionship, to help him hunt.

The rain stopped. The dark clouds parted and the moon shone full, revealing the swaying branches, the little bush that was almost torn from the ground, the tree that lay on its side, its roots stretching towards the sky, the rubble of rock that had fallen from the hill above him, and ended its downward plunge against the giant trunk that now lay lengthways. Deep under that his mother lay buried.

He had been safe in the den she had annexed, and had seen the mountain tumble and trap her as she came home to him, a baby rabbit in her mouth. He no longer trusted the high hills.

He had not known that trees could move, and he watched the tumbled giant, afraid it might rise and walk and fall again and crush him. The night was wild with the wind's hate. The world was storm-bound, the enormous unseen power dominating the hillside.

Below him the moon shone on the wild waters of the loch, foam flung high, the waves ripping across the surface, a restless tumble, forcing themselves towards the rocky outfall where the fall surged downwards, filling the air with a thunderous rushing that drowned even the wind at times.

The cat left the area and found shelter on another hill. Here there was only heather; no trees to threaten him. He found little food and wandered again, down through the glen, moving stealthily, crouched against the ground, always in cover. He learned about traps as well as about guns.

He found a trap with a domestic cat caught in it by the leg. She had died there, unable to free herself, and nobody had come to ease her torment. Hidden deep in the brambles he watched the giant walk up to the metal gin, open it, and throw the body down in disgust.

That was not the prey the man had hoped to find. He knew there was a wild cat on his hill and that he sought. This was a neighbour's cat; perhaps as much of a threat, but it was not his wanted quarry.

He did not want to lose his birds. He kept bantams, and also a pen of rabbits and grouse which he used when training his dogs not to riot. A cat could so easily climb the wire.

The weather was cold and growing colder. The cat, who had been born in high summer and never known winter's chill, fluffed his fur to trap warm air and crouched closer to the wall of his shelter. It offered little warmth.

He watched the moon travel across the sky. He watched the surface of the puddle in front of him glisten and harden, until there was no water left to drink. Only a sheet of glittering hardness that froze his tongue.

He curled up closer on himself, enduring the cold. Cold that hurt his paws, so that he licked them to warm them. Cold that threatened him, so that he rose and stretched and walked outside, but the wind seized him and threw him flat against the rock.

There was nothing left but endurance. He lay, while the light went out again, hidden by tumbling clouds, and the wind went mad.

He had never seen hail. The great stones bounced with a rattle that terrified him. He was even more terrified when one of the iceballs hit his shoulder, bruising him. The cave was no longer safe.

He fled through the night, the storm's bullets battering him, and found a great hole in the tree trunk that lay with its branches in the air. He crept inside, down into the hollow, away from the blinding balls that drummed on the trunk, and covered the ground with white.

He had been pounded and bruised even in that short run. He lay listening, feeling fear creep over him, understanding nothing of the gale that savaged the whole country, felling trees, tearing slates and tiles from roofs, and causing panic everywhere.

Alone, the cat lay and learned that this strange place into which he had been born could threaten him with unseen enemies as well as those that walked on two legs or on four.

The rough wood held his body tightly. There was little space. There were smells of other creatures that had sheltered here, but they had gone, fleeing from the tree when it crashed to the ground.

At last, exhausted, the young cat slept, an uneasy sleep from which he woke again and again, eyes wide, ears pricked, listening for danger. He could not hear danger for the roaring of the wind. He could not see or smell danger. He could do nothing but wait and long for light, and peace from the buffeting wind.

Morning came with a surge of foam on the edge of the loch below him; with rolling sleek waves that hurled against the edging rocks and shattered into shining plumes that frothed into a clear blue sky.

He prowled the beach, keeping out of reach of the clawing sea. There were fish in the pools that the tide had left, and he sat alert, eyes bright and interested, watching them. A pounce, and he clawed at them. Only mouthfuls but they eased the fierce hunger.

They were salty and he went to drink at the burn that trickled slowly, edged with ice. The ice bit his paws. It cracked and broke, so that he wet his fur.

He retreated to the uneasy shelter of the hollow tree, and licked frantically at his pads to warm them. Winter still gripped, and food was hard to find. Cold was a frequent companion, so that he learned to find the snuggest hiding places, deep in the rocky cracks that were almost caves, out of the chill of the wind.

He learned that water vanished under a rock-hard surface that betrayed his paws if he walked on it so that he slid.

He learned that little creatures died of cold and if he found their bodies soon, he could feed without hunting.

He learned that humans vanished when the strange patchlights clicked off, and their homes were silent. There were bins to raid, and there was bounty often in the bins. A meat bone, or a chicken carcase. Food!

One bright morning, when snow had come and gone again, the cat crouched, huddled into his fur, watching light tip the mountains with a glare of red. Far above him, the eagle screamed. He and his mate were everlastingly circling, watching the hidden stir in the undergrowth, ready to dive, ready to kill. They were busy repairing their nest for the coming spring.

The young cat had seen them kill; had heard the dying wails of their unlucky prey and knew that when the sweeping shadow darkened the ground, he must hide and lie close, never betraying his presence with ear twitch or paw flick,

13

holding his breath until the enemy had gone.

Death came fast on the mountain and few had a second chance.

A young rabbit, unwary, and heady with delight after a night of terror, ended his life in the eagle's talons. The young cat watched the shadow grow huge, as the bird fell from the skies.

The cat heard the death note. Saw the shadow change shape, and then, as the bird rose, and began to fly towards his home, the dark shape moved swiftly, until it was only a memory and peace lay on the hill.

The wind had died with the dawn. Only a soft memory of it rustled the grasses, and blew last year's dead leaves. The young cat crept out of his hiding place, and stretched, luxuriating in movement.

The surge of water falling down the steep rocks drowned the footfall behind him. The padding fox had seen the little cat. The fox was hungry. He had eaten nothing but roots and peelings thrown out onto a compost heap, and a few worms. Inside was a gaping void, and though he knew that cats were not beasts to challenge, his aching stomach led him into folly.

The young cat, crouched, watching the ground himself for the telltale ripple of mouse in the grass, listening for the shivering patter of tiny paws, did not see the fox.

The fox had crept behind him, knowing that the scent of cat came to him on the wind and the wind itself would betray nothing.

He pounced.

The cat felt the tremor in the ground and, swifter than heartbeat, turned and raked with angry claws across the fox's face. The cat had not paused to think. He was all urgent instinct, intent on preserving his life.

The vicious slash tore open the skin above the intruder's eyes. Blood blinded him, and, pawing at his face, he ran off, unable to see well enough to fight.

He retreated high on the hill, dabbing continuously at the red that masked his eyes. It was a severe wound, and it was hours before the bleeding stopped. The fox carried the marks across his forehead to his dying day, and those who saw him named him Slash, and wondered how he came by his injuries.

The cat sat, quivering, in the aftermath of terror, his ears flicking to and fro, listening for another telltale sign. He moved away, to an edge of rock, a small overhang, where nothing could come on him from behind, and licked angrily at his fur. The fox had bitten.

His tabby fur was fluffed, his tabby tail was an enormous bush and he snarled softly to himself, angered, and afraid. He was unaware of death, as threatening himself, yet knew of it. Knew that he must not relax guard for a second. Eagle in the sky, fox on the ground, man with his gun, all of them enemies.

He too was hungry. The fox had hit him hard on the shoulder, and his teeth had sunk deep. The young cat tried to lick the wound, but it was in an awkward place and he could not reach it, either with tongue or paw.

It stiffened and lamed him, and for a few days it was not easy to catch his food. Movement hurt. The wound festered, and would not heal. He could not hunt. His injury had slowed him, and he had little to eat but grass and wandering beetles and they did not fill.

He remembered the food in the cottage garden on the hill that was his first home. He limped back to the place that had killed his mother. There he took shelter, unseen, and unheard, his presence unknown to the occupant, though not to her cat.

The old cat was afraid of this young intruder and gave the shed where he lay hidden a wide berth. At night he crept out and stole the cat's food, and once or twice helped himself to a wandering chick. There was water in the bowl left always for the birds.

It was fourteen days before he was strong enough to leave his refuge and even then he bedded near, and returned to raid the plate that was left every night, so devotedly.

He did not trust humans. He fed, and bounded away. Sometimes he lay near, watching for the old woman, knowing her shape, the long black skirt, the purple cardigan, a hole in the elbow, the untidy grey hair.

He always waited until she had left

the garden and the back door was safely shut. Sometimes he lost his meal to the cat; sometimes to the fox who also knew of this unlooked for bounty.

The young cat avoided even the ground where the fox had eaten. He had his own corner, near the great clumps of catmint that bloomed in summer and in which all cats loved to roll. He had not yet discovered that delight.

The cat knew of his presence, and fled at the rank smell of him, and the fox, when the cat was there, made a detour and did not come to the garden.

When darkness came, and the moon fled high among the racing clouds, and the dogs bayed in the village, the cat waited until the lights in the scattered houses had flicked off, and all was still.

Winter clamped the land. Wild storms savaged the hills. The young cat hid from the rain as best he could, shivered with frosts, and licked hurting paws when the ground was rock hard and glassy with ice.

One late April night was colder than any he had known. The wicked killer ice froze on fur and whiskers, froze his plumed breath, and chilled him so much that he fled and took shelter again among the sacks in the outhouse where the old lady kept her garden stores. It lay against the chimney wall and was always warm.

The cat pushed the door, which was unlocked, pawed at it, opening it, and crept inside. He lay against the warm wall, wary, and when dawn came he slipped out again and was lost among the bracken long before his unknowing hostess woke.

He was now a full grown cat, at the height of his youth and strength, and in the past eight months he had learned a great deal about the world in which he lived. He needed a mate.

But he did not know that that was what he needed.

2

THE journey seemed endless. The car was hot and the road stretched on for ever. Kate's ankle hurt. She had twisted it the week before, jumping awkwardly off a piece of apparatus in the gym.

There was such a lot of time to think, to watch the road unwinding in front of her, the towns giving place to the countryside. Fields with sheep and cattle, and an occasional horse, tossing his mane in the wind.

Kate wondered how she would like living in the middle of nowhere. "Happy?" her father asked, as he had asked so often and so anxiously, ever since that dreadful day. She had been sitting at the top of the stairs, huddled into herself, frightened by the solemn voices.

She had been in bed when the policeman rang the bell. There was a woman police constable with her. Her mother had been driving home late, from

20

visiting her grandmother, who had been ill. The road had been icy. The car had skidded, and ended in the river.

That had been over a year ago, but the memory of that night was still vivid, coming to her suddenly when she least expected it, raising a lump in her throat, bringing unwelcome tears. She had to be brave for her father's sake.

It was safer to close her eyes and pretend to sleep now. Her voice would betray her. She heard her father sigh. He sighed so often these days. She couldn't remember when he had last laughed.

She shifted in her seat, moving her head. Her neck was stiff and her ankle ached. She glanced at him through dense lashes. His hands were clenched on the steering wheel, gripping it tightly. Every inch of him seemed stiff, unable to relax. His mouth was set hard, and in his eyes was the lost look she had come to dread. He was concentrating fiercely on the road ahead.

Kate loved to make up stories. Her own misery was easier to bear if it were a story of which she were a part. There would be a happy ending. Everything would come right. Maybe Sir Galahad would come wooing her, riding on a white charger, with a scarlet saddle and silver reins. She was re-reading the Round Table legends, and found refuge from harsh reality in the tales of knights and their ladies, of quests and jousts and tournament.

"His strength was as the strength of ten, because his heart was pure," Kate murmured dreamily.

"What did you say?" Her father negotiated a long incline, and overtook a tractor that had been holding them back for some miles. His voice was startled.

"Nothing," Kate said, alarmed to find she had spoken out loud.

She stretched. Her jeans were too tight. Her tee shirt strained against a newly developing chest. Nothing seemed to fit properly. Even her shoes hurt. Her father's clothes never seemed to look right these days either.

"We'll stop for a meal when we find a decent place," her father said.

Kate looked out at the hedges that seemed to be slipping past them, as if the road were moving and the car standing still. Her mother had died on a January evening. They had never said goodbye to her while she was alive. The betraying lump was coming back and Kate thought determinedly of lambs in the fields and daffodils in the bright gardens.

Now it was spring. New leaf on the trees and the hedgerows were a vivid incredible green. The houses vanished and the road wound lazily through densely wooded hills. The etched branches were hazy, silvery buds smoking on the trees.

Sir Galahad rode in those woods. No sound but the whisper of the wind, the rustle of a skirt, and the soft beat of the hooves on the turf.

"My princess," he'd say. He would bend over her and look into her eyes and not see plain Kate, thirteen years old, with straight dark hair and grey-green eyes, and a sullen mouth that seemed, these days, to want to do nothing but cry.

She would be as beautiful as her mother who had been a dark beauty, though only in her daughter's and her husband's eyes. Mysterious eyes and silken hair, and slim hands.

"Pale hands, pink tipped beside the Shalimar."

Kate knew she had not remembered the right words. She had been so small then, and she dared not ask her father to repeat them for her. Her mother had sung that song so often. But that seemed to be in another life, so very long ago. Life had been wonderful then, with Gramma and Gramper coming to visit, with her mother always at home, though often at her typewriter, writing the stories that she sent to magazines that sometimes printed them.

"One day I'll write a bestseller. You'll see," she had often said, and Kate had laughed and read the stories over her mother's shoulder and been quite sure that one day she would be the daughter of a very famous authoress.

Then her father would come in from his studio, swing her high in his arms and laugh at her.

"How's my gorgeous princess?"

Now she was a thirteen-year-old lump, and no longer a dainty seven-year-old. It was years since he had been able to swing her high. Gramma had died when she was only five years old; Gramper two years later. Then her mother had died. She was terrified that her father would die too, and she would be left alone with no one to look after her.

If only this journey would end. There was too much time to think. Her father had come home a few days before, and begun sorting through his files, and then had taken out his precious cameras and film equipment, which he hadn't used since her mother's death.

"She's still here, all the time. In every room, in everything we do. We need to go away," her father said. "We can go to Gramper's cottage. I've had a piece of real good fortune. A special job; I applied for it and got it. I thought it would be ideal for us, but I can't tell you about it. It's top secret, an incredible piece of luck as the old cottage is the perfect base."

Scotland had been a long way away from home and she had only been to the cottage once, as a tiny girl. Gramper was a vet, with a big country practice, mostly of farm animals.

"I let it after Gramper died. To an old lady whose husband had died, so that she lost her tied farm cottage. I don't think you ever met her but I knew her well when I was a boy." He sighed. "Everything's so different. Poor old Bridie died too, soon after she rented the cottage from me. Mrs McKie has been looking after it for me. She suggested last year that it was a pity to leave it empty, so I asked her to furnish it so that it would be suitable for holiday-makers. I heard about this job before I had a chance to let it. It was just as well we hadn't advertised it yet."

He walked over to the window and stared out of it, but Kate was sure he saw nothing beyond the pane. At least he was talking to her. He went on in the defeated monotone that never seemed to take life.

"It would be silly to stay anywhere else, when we own that."

He sighed.

"Nothing ever works out the way you plan."

Kate knew that his thoughts were of their honeymoon, spent in Scotland while Gramper was away. Long ago, before she was even born. It was odd to think of her

26

parents living and her not there at all.

She had, at first, jumped at the thought of the cottage. There might be ponies in the village that she could ride. She would have to take a very long bus ride to the school, but that would be an adventure.

There was a new life ahead.

She had left all her friends behind, and memories that still hurt. Maybe in a new place she would forget them.

The road twisted to reveal a fairytale scene. A turreted castle set in green lawns, with great trees behind it, towering against the sky. A blue lake, sun glinting on water brushed with foam where the wind teased the wave tops. A giant willow gazing at its own reflection and a golden dog lying at the bottom of a flight of steps that curved towards a great studded oak door that stood invitingly open.

An almost hidden sign at the road edge proclaimed HOTEL.

Kate looked at it, delight in her eyes. "It really is like a fairy story," she said. "Can we stop and eat here? Please?"

Her father looked down at her, and

27

then at the scene beyond them. Behind the towers dark mountains reached for the sky.

"Suppose they put us in the dungeons?" he said, but his voice was light and amused, almost like the old days, and Kate felt a stirring of interest and excitement that had been absent for so long.

She was too anxious to move and the seat belt refused to unlock. Then the catch flew apart and she opened the door, and climbed out onto the forecourt.

The dog rose slowly. A Golden Retriever, regal, his plumed tail waving from side to side. He came to her, and carefully, meticulously, began to inspect her, sniffing her shoes and her legs and her hands. She passed his test and his tail waved more eagerly.

He walked beside her as she climbed the steps and she was no longer Kate in tight jeans that pinched her and a grubby tee shirt stretched too tight, but Princess Kate, elegant and mysterious, her faithful hound at her side, meeting her Prince.

It was easier to face people when she pretended. To blank out the questions they asked in all innocence if they hadn't met her before.

"Yes, dear, of course Kate can stay to tea. Perhaps she'd better ring her mother first, though. She might worry."

It hurt. It was so difficult, still, to say, "No one will worry. My father's at work and my mother's dead. I'm a latchkey kid." She hated going home to the empty house. It was warm in winter with central heating but it wasn't the same. No one to call out to; no smells of baking; or the tap tap tap of the typewriter. No one to listen to the saga of her day, and laugh at the funny things and commiserate over unfairness.

The stories she made up helped to soothe the pain. Her writer mother had passed on something of herself, but Kate was unaware of that.

The castle was enchanting. The great rooms, the elegant furniture, the framed pictures of times long gone, induced a mood of unreality in both of them. Kate, watching her father run up the steps, turned to meet him, a royal lady greeting a courtier.

She watched her father come towards her, and looked at him as if she had never seen him before. They were standing by a full-length mirror, and the spell was broken. She saw a tall distinguished man, untidily dressed, and, beside him, dwarfed by his height, a girl in scruffy clothes with a mop of untidy dark hair, lacking a cut, with an unremarkable face and dark eyes set in wide sockets that slanted like a cat's. All eyes and no face. Kate hated her face.

"You need clothes that fit," her father said, startled out of his misery by her reflected image. "We'll buy you some before we get to Tigh-na-Bhet."

"Are we really going to live in the middle of nowhere? How could Gramper work from such a lonely place?" Kate asked.

"The cottage isn't really so isolated; it just seems so," her father said. "Farming vets don't work at home, and Gramper could easily travel in his Land-Rover. It's only a short walk to the shops. Well, only a mile and a half, when the river hasn't flooded at the ford. A longer walk over the hills. There's a bus that passes about a mile away three times a week."

It sounded like the end of the world.

The waitress who came to their table was plump and smiling, with a gentle Scottish lilt that Kate found hard to follow until she grew used to it.

"Salmon straight from the river; new potatoes; petit pois; broccoli. Sound good, Kate?" Her father's voice was anxious, needing her approval for this extravagance.

"Lovely," Kate said. She was hungry. She hoped her father would enjoy this meal. He hadn't been eating much at all lately. They had taken it in turns to cook, often convenience foods as they didn't need complicated recipes or preparation. If you put them in the microwave and did exactly as it said on the packet they turned out well.

"Our last decent meal," Gavin McKendrick said. "We'd better buy a good recipe book, or we'll have to live on porridge. And the way I cook, that will be burnt with big lumps in it."

Kate smiled. Her father was exaggerating. Nothing they ate was ever burnt, though it wasn't always very appetising and they went out far too often to the Chinese takeaway or the chippy.

"No takeaways where we're going. We'll both have to learn to cook more adventurously."

The table was by the window, looking out over the lake. The wind stirred the leaves of the willow and the dog was back at his post. There were soft heaped clouds in a pastel sky. An unreal scene, a watercolour painted by a romantic artist who loved the world.

If only life were like that.

In spite of her worries about loneliness Kate enjoyed her meal, and the lemon cheesecake that followed the salmon was light as a kitten's breath.

"I'd like to stretch my legs. How's that ankle?" Gavin asked.

Kate made a face.

"Sore. I can sit by the water and wait for you. I'd like to stroke the dog. Can we have a dog when we get to Scotland?"

"We're already there," her father said,

smiling at her. "I don't think a dog would do, do you? Not with moors all round us. And no fences."

"Can't we fence it?"

"We'll see, love."

Kate watched him walk down the steps and turn beside the lake, his figure growing smaller. She felt very alone. Suppose he died too?

She limped towards the carved seat by the lake and whistled to the dog. He came to her, welcoming her with dignity. He settled at her feet, his undemanding presence comforting her.

She didn't want to sit still. The wind was cool. Kate signalled to the Retriever, and walked slowly round the lake margin. There were two swans courting, bowing and raising their wings. Ducks swam lazily. At the far side she knelt, her arms round the warm solid body, burying her head in his fur. His brown eyes watched her, as if he offered sympathy.

The dog, sensing her misery, licked the tears away. She held him tightly, longing for a dog of her own.

At last the tears stopped and she washed her face in the water, the dog watching her, a puzzled wrinkle on his forehead.

She stuffed her sodden hankie into her pocket and stood up.

Her father had been lost in his own thoughts as he walked, the lonely ache returning. Today was April 30th. They had been married on April 28th. The second anniversary since his wife had died. The first had been three months after the accident. She always made such an occasion of all anniversaries; of birthdays, and of Christmas.

He had not reminded Kate of the date, but she had remembered. She watched him come towards her, walking slowly, all the bounce gone from his step. He used to run everywhere, and laugh so often.

"Ready?" he asked, as she met him.

She nodded, and knelt to kiss the dog goodbye. He licked her and stood, tail waving, watching the car drive out into the road and turn towards the distant hills.

"Only about two hours' drive now," Gavin said.

Kate lifted the box of cassettes, looking for music. Something she remembered from long ago and there it was.

"I love looking across the sea to Skye," Gramper had said, in the safe days when they were all together. "There's tangle on the beach. A healing smell. When I'm low, I bring back strands of the bright orange wrack so that I can smell it close to me. And I play the music of the islands."

She clipped the cassette into its space, and turned the sound on.

The music eased the silence, bringing memories of Gramper himself, of him holding her tightly, and of peace. And her mother's soft voice singing with the music.

The deep voice, with its velvety overtones, soared into the air. Kate listened dreamily, as she had listened long ago, safe on Gramper's knee. He had given her a cassette player for her birthday and the songs he brought her were Scottish.

They always hummed softly with the music until the last lines when his cracked old voice rang out in triumph and drowned the singer.

If ye're thinking in your inner heart
    the braggart's in ma step,
Then ye've never smelt the tangle of
    the Isles.

It went something like that. The tangle. The healing weed, drifting in for ever from the restless sea, to lie on the sandy beaches, and dry under the sun. Would it heal them?

And then they were there. The winding lane crept through heather slopes that would later be in flower. Sheep stared at them and then bent their heads to graze. They lambed late here in the hills and the small beasts watched them with curious faces. A Highland cow and her calf blocked the road briefly, the shaggy beast lowering her horns as if she would charge the car.

Her father did laugh then, and hooted, and both beasts moved. "They're fairly timid, so don't worry," he said, as Kate looked back anxiously, wondering if these huge cattle would be roaming round their cottage. The calf was adorable, but the mother looked menacing. "Just keep away from their babies."

Round a steeply angled corner, the engine protesting, and they were there.

Her father looked at the overgrown garden, sighing.

"I ought to have seen that someone came to keep it neat," he said. "It looks so neglected. I hope it's better inside."

The cottage was smaller than she remembered. Four rooms downstairs and three up; an added kitchen with a bathroom above it. A generator that was housed in a new shed, and that sprang into grumbling life after her father had attacked it with more energy than knowledge.

Outside was an outhouse, and when Kate looked inside she saw that it had once been a stable. The surgery had been here, she remembered, and there were still kennels. It was beginning to show signs of disuse, but the memory of its busy days was still there. The shelves that had housed the medicines and his instruments. The cupboards and the filing cabinet, although that was now empty, except, surprisingly, for a small pile of dusters, and a dustpan and brush, all new and unused.

The kennel compound was overgrown with weeds. She could clear it. A place to keep a dog.

The cottage was high on the side of the hill, a huge rocky cliff sheltering it. The garden was angled steeply, rising many feet above their heads, and sloping down to the loch below, where the wind laced the wavetops with white.

There were beds to air, and to make; a meal to prepare. Their lavish lunch was only a memory and Kate was suddenly and savagely hungry again. She pushed the hair out of her eyes as she faced the wind outside, and then came back to peel potatoes and grill bacon, and add a tin of baked beans.

The brown bread they had bought on the way was crusty and nutty to taste.

The meal over, her father went outside to discover whether there was wood for the stove, while Kate explored the cottage.

It was sparsely furnished and needed to be made far more homelike, but Kate wasn't going to complain. Her father's freelance work was unpredictable and if an assignment came, he had to take it, never mind what other arrangements were made. This was the first time he had been able to include her on one of his engagements. He had turned so many down since her mother died, so that she would be able to stay at home, and not have to go away and stay with people they barely knew.

Looking at the cane chairs with their big ugly cushions, Kate thought longingly of home. White walls. Patterned curtains that she hated on sight.

It was fine for a short holiday, a place to sleep and leave at dawn for fishing, and return to eat and sleep again. No ornaments. No pictures.

Kate knew that she would not have chosen the colours, but it was a place to live, even if it seemed like a temporary home. Maybe she could change that.

"One day we might have a new home," her father had said. Their furniture was in store. Scotland was a staging post, and soon they would move on.

Across the creaming water the Cuillins reared out of misty clouds. Over the sea to Skye.

Later that evening, the curtains drawn,

the generator throbbing, a constant background, the cassette player singing to them of misty islands and men who marched to pipes and drums, peace touched both father and daughter.

They sat together on the settee, watching the smoky flames dancing in the fire, which Gavin had banked with peat, remembering the old ways and the hot embers and the warmth it gave. The night was chilly.

Kate leaned against her father, feeling safe and loved.

"Mummy liked dogs," she said.

Gavin smiled to himself. His daughter had all her mother's wiles.

"Pups need house training; and need company; and I won't be able to take one around with me. I'll be very busy. And you'll be at school. It wouldn't be fair, love."

Kate sighed. She stood and stretched herself and went to the window, lifting the curtain to look out at the dark.

"There are lights further up the hill. I wonder who lives there?" she asked.

Gavin joined her. "We'll soon find out, from the postman or someone like that. Everyone knows everyone else in a small place and the postman will know them all."

It was the postman who was their first visitor, three days later, bringing mail for both of them. Kate was sitting on a rock, looking down at the sea. Her father had gone out on some mysterious errand.

"No, love, I can't take you with me. Not yet. Later, maybe," he had said.

She was glad to see the little red van. This was a very lonely place, as lonely as she had feared. The postman, small and plump and red-headed, with a wicked glint of laughter in his eyes, brought her two letters and a tiny parcel, addressed to her father.

"It's a lovely view, but it needs people," he said. "Wouldn't do for me. I like a house in a street and people to watch and noise all round me." He brought a bar of chocolate out of his pocket and broke it in two, handing one half to Kate, before sitting himself down on a nearby rock.

"We were all sorry to hear about your mother," he said.

"Thank you," Kate said, and for the

first time it wasn't too difficult to think about it.

"Ah, well, it happens," the man said. "Ma mother died when I was a wee lad. I don't even remember her."

He bit into the chocolate and looked down at the water. "There's otters there, and beasts on the hill, and plenty of company with the birds as well."

Kate had not thought of that kind of company. The chocolate was dark and bitter, an unusual flavour that tasted good.

"Will you be staying long?"

"I think so," Kate said. "My father has a lot of work to do here; and we've sold our old house. We didn't want to stay there."

"And what work would that be?" the man asked.

Kate stared at him, embarrassed.

"I don't really know." It sounded as if she were putting him off. "He doesn't talk to me a lot, not since Mum died," she said, hoping that would cover the awkwardness.

The man nodded.

"A thing like that, it takes an awful

long time to get over," he said, accepting her explanation, though that did not stop him speculating about it later to the butcher, over a pint in the Vaults.

"Who lives on the hill above us?" Kate asked, wanting to change the conversation.

"Old Mairi Douglas. They say she has the healing touch, with herbs and potions. She helps the mothers with the bairns when they are ill. She's a good woman, is Mairi. A good neighbour, ye'll find her."

He stood up, yawning.

"I must be on my way. I hope ye'll both be verra happy here."

His soft burr was soothing. Kate watched the van vanish down the winding trail, growing smaller and smaller.

There was movement behind her. A whisper on the wind, of small paws padding, a half-seen shape in the grass, a rumour of a tabby tail, of a head turning and a piercing glance from green slant eyes.

She tried to see into the shifting heather, but only the wind was there to mock her.

The young cat had come to forage, as there were always mice round the deserted cottage. He had been startled to find people there, and had hidden. He needed to get back on the hill, out of danger.

He also needed food and he had smelled fish cooking. Kate had put it to cool on the sill, intending to make fish cakes for the next day's breakfast. The window was wide.

The cat, passing, took only a moment to leap up, snatch the now cold fish and vanish. Kate, staring, later, at the empty dish and the tell-tale marks on the cloth beside it, of padded paws, knew she had been right.

There *had* been a cat in the grass.

Perhaps it belonged to the old woman in the cottage above them. Perhaps it was a wild cat. Perhaps she could tame it. Her father couldn't object to a cat. Could he?

All the same, she felt it was wiser not to tell him, and merely said she had burned the fish and had to throw it away. Later, they would go down to the loch and catch more.

That night, unable to sleep, and sure there was something about outside the cottage, Kate went to the window and looked down. The cat, silvered by moonlight, was crouched in the grass, watching. He did not see her. She thought she had never seen so beautiful an animal.

If she couldn't have a dog, she would have a cat, and here was the animal she needed. He would be company. He was glorious. From that moment, she was obsessed.

3

SHEINA McDONALD had very recently come to teach at the school which all the older children went to at thirteen. She was young, and this was only her second post since she had left college.

She was taller than the other women on the staff. Red curly hair complimented a heart-shaped face with grey-green eyes, and a stubborn chin warned the perceptive that her character belied her appearance.

Her mouth caught many a man's eye, but the lines of her face were sad. Those who met her briefly were amazed on the rare occasions when she relaxed into a vivid smile that transformed her face.

She had left Scotland for England and taught for three years in a big comprehensive school in a city. A love affair gone sour, followed by homesickness, drove her back to her native hills when her mother died.

46

She had intended to sell the little cottage on the burnside, where she had grown up. Her father had been a gamekeeper on the big estate and when the old Laird died and the place was sold, had been able to buy the cottage for a very small sum, under the terms of his employer's will. It was remote, but not too remote, and Sheina's B registration car gave her mobility.

The cottage gave her a base, a home of her own, instead of the small and unlovely apartments she had inhabited over the past few years. Instead of mean streets there were the high hills, the heather and the soft murmur of the little burn, and a peace she had forgotten.

She felt old and sad and wise, and her colleagues found her prickly and very wary of men.

"Like a startled hind," the art master said, after a vain attempt to persuade her to join him for an evening meal. "Such a waste," he added, thinking of long legs, and bright hair and shadowed eyes that had stared at him frostily, and then looked away.

When Kate started school, Sheina was

her form mistress. The woman knew of the child's background, of her mother's death in a road accident, and thought she looked forlorn.

The child wore the oddest clothes at times, chosen with little care for anything except serviceability, and in colours that did not suit her. Nothing ever seemed to fit.

Kate responded to the sympathy that was hidden, never expressed, and liked her form mistress. She missed the long talks she had had with her mother, the laughter, the silly little jokes.

Her father was always busy with his work, so that he was frequently abstracted. He was even more solemn these days.

He was often out, his camera always with him. He was, she was sure, building a hide somewhere, but she dared not ask. He was filming for a television documentary, he had told her, but nobody was to know. He did not want anyone to guess where he went, or what he did.

Kate wondered at the secrecy and resented it. It was hard to fend off Miss

McDonald's questions, though she was sure that her teacher wasn't prying. Just interested, and Kate longed for someone who was interested in her.

She felt too isolated to respond. Her classmates were suspicious of her, an outsider coming in late to their school, and she had no desire to be branded as teacher's pet.

Her mother had been English and Kate had not picked up her father's Scottish burr, now faint after years away from home. Her accent sounded alien, even to herself. Nobody else spoke like her, not even Miss McDonald, and sometimes the other children mimicked her, mocking her.

She was embarrassed when Miss McDonald spoke to her, saying 'good afternoon' in her soft brogue, the 'a' sound short, as it was in cat. Kate always said 'good arfternoon' with the 'a' long. If she said it her way, she felt as if she were correcting her teacher, but if she said it the other way, then she was mimicking. So she mumbled, giving the impression that she was far too shy to speak at all.

Kate knew it was silly to worry; there

were so many other things to worry about, but that one loomed largest of all as it was a daily occurrence. She was also very aware of her odd clothes, bought by her father for her to 'grow into' so that everything was too long and too large.

He himself had little use for clothes other than to keep him decent, and always wore jeans and old sweaters that, though clean, were in need of mending. Kate mended them as best she could. When he went to the village in the battered old soft top Land-Rover he was conspicuous in the shabby camouflage jacket that made him look like a soldier, off duty.

The villagers thought of them as two waifs, cast up like flotsam on the loch shores.

"It's no life for a lassie," the postmaster said, when Sheina went in to buy food for the school cat, that had adopted her as its owner. It lived in the school pavilion, and hunted industriously, so that nobody wanted to turn it away. A big purring tabby, with a thoughtful expression and long remarkable white whiskers. Kate had also adopted it, and often sought its company in her lonely breaks and lunch hours.

"Does he speak much when he comes in here?" Sheina asked, curious about the child's father, disliking him for his apparent neglect of his daughter.

"He asks for what he needs and doesna talk at all. He's a dour man," the postmaster said, putting down five tins of catfood on the counter. "That will be one pound and fifty pence, if you please, Miss McDonald. The school cat should be verra healthy on what ye buy for him."

"He's bonny," Sheina said, and the postmaster expanded to her sudden vivid smile. "He's a big fellow, and beautiful. The children love him, and he loves them."

"And will ye no be eating yourself this week?" the postmaster asked, as Sheina turned away, her eyes following a tall figure that stalked past the door.

"That's Kate's father. I've a good mind . . ." she hesitated, watching the man stride up the street and out of sight.

"Best no' to interfere. The child is

well, and she's fed, and she's no more unhappy than any other child would be without a mother."

Sheina, bringing her mind back to butter and sugar and coffee and cheese and milk, put the thought from her mind. Maybe he would come to the parents' evening and she could speak to him then.

Maybe she could persuade him to let her take Kate and buy her some prettier clothes. It had been easier in the days when uniform was compulsory. Everyone looked the same then. The child would be better in jeans and tee shirts and jerseys than those old-fashioned too long skirts and the white blouses that looked as if they had come from a shop devoted to grandmother's discards.

Her anorak was a small version of her father's, bought from the boys' department of the local store. The man had no idea . . .

The days seemed endless. Kate, too shy to break into any of the small groups of friends, tended to go off alone at break and at lunch time, find herself a quiet corner and read a book. Books were safe.

She could lose herself. Could dream of being grown up and rich and famous.

Sometimes, when one of her classmates had been exceptionally unpleasant, she imagined herself with power over them, perhaps to give them a job, or to help them in their chosen career.

She refused, watching them lose heart, lose confidence. And then, when they were at their lowest in spirits, in total despair, she reached out a hand and helped them up again, earning their undying gratitude.

One of her favourite stories was that of Cuchulain, the Hound of Ulster, that had saved his master's life so often, had battled with him through danger and disaster. The English mistress, a tall sombre individual, near to retirement, named Kipperfeet because of her long thin shoes, chided her for reading tales meant for much younger children.

Kate could never tell her how the thought of the faithful Hound excited her. Miss Heynon would never have understood.

She cried over the story of Gelert, who fought the wolf that got into the castle while his owner was hunting. The brave dog saved his master's baby. But the prince, finding the overturned cradle and bloodstained bedding, plunged his sword into the dog. Then, too late, found the mauled body of the savage raider and the unharmed child.

If only she could have a puppy. Or a kitten. Or even a rabbit or a hamster, something warm and furry to cuddle and love. Her father never cuddled her, and, alarmed by the news coverage of child abuse, did not even kiss his daughter any more. He stayed aloof from her, bothered unduly by the fear that he might be accused of harming her, if anyone saw him showing affection towards her. Life had served him badly and grief had made him over anxious in every direction where Kate was concerned.

Yet he couldn't show her he cared. He didn't know how.

Kate, unaware of adult concerns, missed the cuddles he had given her when her mother was alive, but never attempted even to ask for a kiss or an arm round her shoulders. Unwittingly, the gulf between them grew.

He was not interested in her childish affairs, or in talking about the books she read. Sometimes he helped her with homework, but encouraged her to battle by herself with problems rather than to run to him to solve them. The world was cruel and when she grew up she would find it crueller and she had to learn to cope.

Once he had thought of life as a challenge, his wife beside him, and more children than Kate. But the children had not come, until a few months before the accident, she had discovered she was pregnant. The child had been a boy, they told him.

The anger spilled over at night, so that often he got up and dressed and went walking on the hills, railing against the Fate that had deprived him of Kate's mother and of his baby son. A son to watch grow up. Kate would have loved the child. She adored babies and had always wanted a brother or sister. She had known of the coming birth, but her grief for that child could never be like his.

Nor could he talk to his daughter. She

was too young to understand any of his concerns. They ate together when he was at home. Polite mealtimes.

"Please pass the salt, daddy. Is your supper all right?"

And he always said yes because she had tried, although the learning was hard and her attempts at ambitious menus sometimes failed, leaving her watching him, wide eyed and anxious, lest he comment on the awfulness of the food.

On the third Sunday of their stay, she waited till her father had left the house, and then slipped out and followed him. Down the hill and along the shore, keeping well out of sight, picking up the trail of his footsteps in the rippled wet sand. Then up a steep cliff, on to the moor, and across the boggy peat, dodging the pools.

She was a spy, on the trail of an enemy agent. She was one of the three musketeers, busy on the Queen's business. She would be rewarded with medals, and riches beyond anyone's dreams. She was a monarch, riding to meet her army.

There was movement above her. She

stopped, and stared at the sky. Blue sky, with small white clouds that dodged about the sun. And there, riding the wind, was the most beautiful bird in all the world.

Light gilded his feathers. He was a soaring monarch, the king of the hills, and Kate knew her father's secret. He was filming an eagle's nest. The Golden Eagle. She watched the great bird flying, and then he banked and wheeled and turned towards the heights, rising until he was as small as a swallow, and then he vanished from her sight.

She knew why he hadn't told her. There was danger for the birds once their presence was known. The nest site had to be secret, or people would come, and maybe steal the eggs. Or even the fledglings. That was why he had not told her, but it hurt Kate to think her father hadn't trusted her. She would have loved to climb too, but that was dangerous, on her own, and she knew that if found out, she would get into serious trouble. She could come here and see the parent birds fly, and maybe see the nestlings when they first took wing. It wasn't the same, seeing it on film. And the birds were so near.

She sat, watching. If only she could see the nest.

She could see the outline of it, far above her, at the edge of a rocky cliff. Her father's hide must be above it, or he would not be able to see the birds at all.

She had to see it; see the baby birds if they were hatched, see the female incubating the eggs, see the great raft of sticks that they made, that her father had told her about. He loved eagles, and had always promised himself that one day he would film them, would learn their secrets and show them to the world.

Could she climb without him seeing her? There was a narrow gully, that looked as if it might be easy for her to reach and would give her cover. It would bring her out above the nest, but hidden from the only place the hide could be, by high overhanging rocks.

She watched her father climbing the rocky hill. Up and up, into the sky, and then she stopped and crouched, and saw

58

him vanish over the little crest. He should have trusted her.

She would never, ever tell. She could be captured by an enemy and tortured, and nothing would drag the information from her. He should have known.

She would hug the knowledge to her, that she too had seen the nest. It would be her secret. He would never guess that she knew all about his film, about the birds nesting high on the hill. She too would watch and one day, when she was grown up, would surprise him. Maybe she'd write a book about the eagles, and her own observations.

The Kings of the Glen by Kate McKendrick. Everyone would read it and they'd see her name in the papers and the reviews would all be splendid, and she'd be famous and perhaps at last her father would be proud of her. And the girls at school would see the book in the bookshops and remember the girl they had laughed at because of her funny accent, and be sorry they hadn't made friends.

The soaring eagle climbed again into the blue, wings spread, a king of the air. He would be hunting for himself and his mate and perhaps for the babies too. She pictured them, ugly still, almost featherless, screaming beaks gaping for food.

Her father had talked of them, so often. She remembered him, sitting by the fire in the big armchair in their old home, his face alight with excitement.

"They're such beautiful birds, Kate, so enormous. Nothing like the sparrows and chaffinches we see here. They live in the high hills, kings of the air. The sun shines on their feathers, gilding them, and they crown the skies."

He had taken her once, when a very little girl, to a falconry centre where they had a Golden Eagle. There had been other eagles too, but this one she had loved. He was a gentle bird, used to being handled, unlike the big Himalayan eagle in the next cage that threatened anyone near with his cruel curved beak and had to be fed by food that was lowered on a pole, or he attacked the feeder.

Goldie had, they thought, been stolen from a nest as a fledgling and reared, very badly, and then sold to a dealer who put him in a cage that was far too small. The people who ran the centre had found him with two broken wings, broken by beating them in vain against the bars of his narrow cage.

Here he had a huge cage and could fly a little, but even so he was a captive bird. He adored being cuddled and lay, absurdly, talons in the air, upside down in the falconer's arms and crooned gently, and happily. When he fed he mantled his wings over his food so that no one could see it.

"He's never quite grown up," they said. They thought he was about four years old. He could never return to the wild as the wings had never healed properly and his flights were slow and clumsy. He could never hunt for himself.

Kate could no longer bear it: she had to see the birds in their natural home. Resentment coloured her feelings. She would go by herself; see for herself, somehow. Her father need never know. If he climbed there daily, loaded with equipment, it couldn't be a difficult ascent.

Ignoring the warnings in her mind, she began to climb.

At first all went well, and she revelled in movement. Up the rock and up again. Handhold, foothold, stop and breathe. She was never afraid of heights and as the ground below her receded, she looked down and saw a rabbit, dwarfed, a toy creature, pause and lift its head and stare at the sky.

And then the bird plunged towards her, down, down, through the air, talons raked towards her face, and she knew it was threatening her.

If she fell . . .

If she stayed . . . she would die, with those tearing claws in her face and her eyes, with those vast wings beating at her. Or she might fall and survive, but blinded, as he raked towards her, nearer and nearer. She could hear the wind in his feathers, the beat of his wings and she was deafened by his wild cries. He hated her, the intruder, threatening his territory.

He was not merely trying to drive her away. She was sure he intended to kill her.

The bird was screaming, terrifying her, daring this intruder to venture nearer to the nest.

"He has babies there. He's afraid I'll take them, or hurt them. He's protecting them," Kate thought despairingly.

The eagle flew away from the gully, and soared, and then once more came that appalling screaming plunge, legs braced, talons outstretched to rake at her face. She clung to the rocks, flattened against them, and felt the wind as he passed her, and then he was below her.

She thought he had gone.

He rose on the airstream, gaining height, only, she realised to plunge again, and fly at her, threatening her, every line of his body showing his outrage at her intrusion.

She thought of her father, somewhere above her, perhaps glorying in this display, busy with his camera, unaware it was his daughter whose life was in danger.

She was going to fall onto the rocks. She was going to be torn by the great talons. She was going to die, stupidly, because she had been too curious, because she had not waited until her father could take her into his confidence, because she had wanted to see the eagles flying free.

Now she was seeing the bird in all its majesty, trying to evict this puny intruder from his kingdom. He plunged again, the wild screeches sounding like the knell of death, and Kate clung to the rock, too terrified to move, not knowing whether it was safer to go up, or go down, or to freeze and pretend she were part of the overhang, and not human at all.

There was no one near to help. Nothing to distract the great bird. There was nowhere to go.

She had never imagined such fear.

4

KATE clung to the rock, pressing against it, her face hidden against the rough stone. At least her eyes would be safe. She felt vulnerable, knowing those great talons could rake the skin away from her body, could flay her to the bone.

The bird flew up into the air, and there was sudden silence, into which crept the throbbing of an engine. Far away, the mountain rescue helicopter was en route to a climbing disaster. Shakily, Kate realised it might have been on its way to her later that day, to pick up her mangled body from the rocks below.

The distant hum of the helicopter grew louder. The eagle, threatened by a creature even bigger than he, flew to sanctuary. Kate could not see the machine, but was grateful for its presence.

All desire to see the nest site had gone. She was cold and trembling. She climbed down from her gully, and made her way back to the shore. She was aware that life was going to be even more difficult now that she knew her father's secret and she had to keep that fact from him.

It would be so easy for her tongue to betray her when she was tired and they were together in the quiet confiding warmth of the log fire that cast shadows across the room.

Could she tell him what she knew? Tell him that she was prepared as he was to keep silence, to guard the safety of the nest, to make sure nobody would ever find it? Though others must see the birds flying and know they were there.

Guilt at following her father needled at her, as she slipped back to the shore, and spent the rest of the morning skimming stones across a glassy sea. Though the sun was warm she still felt cold, and the memory of that screaming beak and the raking talons and beating wings would haunt her dreams for weeks to come.

She had forgotten that eagles were so huge. On the ground, wings folded, Goldie had looked a much smaller bird. She had never seen him above her with wings outstretched. His shadow had covered her, blotting out the sun. No wonder the small beasts fled when the hawk shadows raced across the ground.

She wished, more and more, that her father would talk to her. She dared not ask where he went, although she knew. She couldn't tell him she knew. Sometimes she slipped after him, and lay on the hillside, watching the eagle soar.

So long as she never tried to climb up to the nest again, she was sure the bird would ignore her. There, in the sky above her, was wild excitement, as the great creature floated effortlessly, or veered in her direction, wings beating, and once passed above her, so that she could see the colours of his feathers, the great talons, the immense body that thrust the air.

She shivered, memory betraying her, and crouched even lower against the ground, as afraid as any bolting rabbit.

She remembered clinging to the rock as he sought to destroy her.

And then, moments later, she heard the scream of a small animal dying and she watched him soar again, a young rabbit held in the cruel hooked talons.

67

Why did some creatures have to die so that others might live? Why did her mother have to die? Better to lose herself again in books. To dream of knights and fair maidens, of dragons and fairytale nonsense because so many modern books seemed to deal with problems like hers or worse and she wanted to forget those, not dwell on them, or suffer with others suffering as she was.

She wanted to escape to a world where life was kind and women were fair and men were handsome and gallant, and there was courtesy and chivalry.

The good knights always defeated the bad knights and the dragons, and the maidens were always rescued and married their saviour, and lived happily ever after.

They didn't die before their time in road accidents leaving motherless children.

She did not want smalltime heroes with clay feet binding them firmly to a squalid world, though she knew the dreams were only dreams and perhaps life had never been like that for anyone.

Sometimes her dreams spilled over into

lesson time, so that she sat, looking out of the window at the busy street beyond the school playground, so different to the quiet heather and bracken-clad hills outside her home, and was in trouble for not concentrating.

"She's a bright child," Sheina said to the games mistress, who was her only confidante. "But she's so quiet, and I can't trigger any spark of life from her. She's too good, too polite, too retiring. Her only fault is that constant dreaminess, as if she were somewhere far away, and not part of the class at all."

"A child like that shouldn't be brought up by a man," Alison Nunn said, her voice tart. She herself was divorced and had a small daughter. Her husband had left her for a much younger and prettier woman and was now raising a second family. Alison had little time for men, having had her confidence completely destroyed. Sheina, herself hurt, found a natural companion in the older woman.

Kate went back often to a silent house, her father almost only a memory, she felt at times. The eggs were due to hatch and he virtually lived up on the hill. Even though she knew why he was there, she longed for his presence, and sometimes wondered if he ever thought about her at all.

She read poetry and read and re-read Tennyson's poem about Mariana in the moated grange. All the desolation and the loneliness:

The broken sheds looked sad and
  strange:
Unlifted was the clinking latch;
Weeded and worn the ancient thatch
Upon the lonely moated grange.

The old stables beyond the cottage were memories of a more affluent time. The slates on the roof were mossed, and hidden, and bracken grew out of one corner of the gutter. The wind whimpered through cracks beneath the doors, and rain came in through the roof, where a slate was missing. No one needed them now.

She waited, it seemed endlessly, for her father's footsteps on the path, for his voice calling as he opened the door, for his presence in the quiet room.

One evening he was much later than usual. The first eaglet had hatched in the night and he had missed the hatching. He was determined not to miss the breaking of the second egg and the emergence of the damp little creature. Its brother or sister might push it out and kill it. He wanted to catch that moment too. There was nothing he could do to alter the course of events.

Kate couldn't settle. She had cooked the evening meal and eaten alone. She looked from the window, longing for the tall figure to stride up the hill towards her, coming from his secret place. She longed for him to greet her as he had when she was small, with a bear hug that squeezed her ribs and took her breath away.

Sometimes she thought she heard a cat calling in the night, but it was weeks before she glimpsed the animal again. He had been hunting on the hill, and caught nothing and was hungry. He remembered there had been food at the cottage, and slipped into cover, watching the house.

That night was very warm and the kitchen window was open. Kate had cooked sausages and mash for supper, and put her father's meal aside on the dresser. She could heat it up for him when he came.

She knelt at the window for a long time, watching the sulky sea throw itself against the shingle, ebb and return, the waves building. The wind was strengthening and by midnight there would be the eternal crash and shock as the water fought the land.

Kate finished her homework and found herself a book. She settled at last to read.

The cat was a silent thief, soft pawed, jumping through the open window, eating quickly, ears pricked for any sound, ready to spring away if someone came into the room.

He was undisturbed, and went back to stretch out under the lee of a rock out of the wind and sheltered from the rain, and sleep, purring, full fed. Kate, going to fetch the plate when her father came in, stared at it. There was nothing left and she had to cook bacon and eggs hastily and serve them with a tin of baked beans, wondering where her father's meal had gone.

"You won't work this weekend?" Kate asked, her voice forlorn. The weekends seemed endless and her father left her on her own for hours.

"We need money to live, Kate," Gavin said. "Money doesn't grow on trees. And I need to make a good job of this film. Then I will be given more work like it, and we can visit other exciting places."

'But it isn't exciting for me,' she thought, but didn't say it. They did need money to live. A lot of money, she realised as it was she who now bought the food, and sometimes her father didn't give her enough and she had to ask him for more.

The postmistress understood, and briefed her husband, so that the child always had a list with her. Kate wrote it carefully, so that she could keep track, and the prices were written against each item, as she bought it. The father seemed to have his head away in the clouds and no idea of what things really cost.

Kate worried sometimes in case she spent more than they had, and Gavin never thought to explain to her that they were not living up to his income, even now. He too was always afraid that the work would cease, that nobody would want his films and he did not know what he would do if that happened. He had no other skill.

Only now did he realise how supportive his wife had been. She had always been there to boost his confidence, to make him laugh, to tease away the many worries as he was a man who worried constantly, seeing danger where none existed.

He had never thought of the real danger that took his wife and unborn son away from him for ever. Now, sometimes, when he was filming, unreasoning terror overtook him, and he was afraid that something had happened to Kate. That she had slipped and fallen on the rocks, or gone swimming and drowned, leaving him totally bereft. And even though the eagles were flying, and he should have been capturing them on film, he left his work and hurried down the hillside, anxious to see her, to make sure she was safe.

Yet when they met, he could not bring himself to hug her. He only nodded at her, and went indoors, to help her with the meal, or to wait for her to dish up.

Kate invented occupations for herself. She explored the rocks and the little pools on the beach, and began to draw the fronded flowerlike sea anemones and the coloured weeds, the fragile green sea lettuce, the bladder wrack, with its swelling pods that popped so satisfyingly when they were dry. To note the little crabs that stood on tiptoe and threatened her with their nippers, waving them furiously at her, so that she laughed at these tiny Lilliputian heroes and felt like Gulliver.

She wandered on the hills, watching the birds soar and wheel. She sat and listened to the endless murmur of the sea, and loved the wild excitement of blustery days when the wind keened round the cottage and the waves crashed against the rocks and spray flew high.

Maybe an arm would rise from the deeps, flashing a sword for a king. Or a mermaid surface and sing to her. Instead, one memorable afternoon, a head did surface, a wise round doglike head, the head of a seal.

Kate kept very still, watching, and the seal seemed to watch her. Then she was aware of movement beyond the rocks. A baby seal lay there, and called mournfully and eerily to his mother. Kate crouched, trying to be a rock, trying to be invisible, and watched as the mother seal came ashore, lumbering clumsily, and her baby waddled to greet her. He began to suck, lying against the vast shape that dwarfed him, and one flipper waved above him, as if protecting him.

She stayed still for a long time, until both went down to the sea again, returning to their own world, so far removed from hers. How did it feel to be a beast of the waves, hunting for fish? Arrowing through the deep waters, seeking food. Did they see the world around them as she did, full of colour and light, or was theirs a different world, half hidden maybe, because their eyes did not see as hers did.

Stiffly, Kate stood up, and began to walk slowly back to the cottage. Somewhere high on the slopes, she heard a bang. Someone was shooting. A hare, or a rabbit maybe. She hated killing for food, yet she ate both meat and fish and could not face a vegetarian diet. It was better to forget how meat came to the table.

The eagle eggs must be hatched. Her father would want to be there to film everything that happened. To see the small beaks gaping for food; to watch how the parents behaved. Did both hunt, or only one? What food did they bring, and how did they prepare it for the babies? There was so much to find out. If only she could be there too. He must be safe in his hide from the angry bird that had tried to destroy her.

The birds had so many enemies. The shepherds, sure that the adult birds took lambs; the gamekeepers, knowing they did take grouse; those who wanted to kill for the pleasure of killing.

Suppose that shot on the hill had been at the eagles? Or at her father? Kate was suddenly afraid, feeling herself surrounded by enemies waiting to pounce on her.

If only she had a dog for company and to protect her. It was too lonely here; only the wide sky and the ever moving sea, and the white birds wheeling and calling, mewing and mournful as they flew.

If only her father would take her too, to watch with him. She wouldn't make a sound, wouldn't disturb him. She suddenly hated the cottage, hated the sea that never stopped its din, hated the world that had taken her mother from them.

There was nowhere to go, and no one to take her. She almost hated her father for his selfishness. He never thought of her feelings, only of his own. He rarely talked, always looking inside himself, planning his filming, his day's work, thinking of the eagles, more important than his daughter.

Kate, her hands clasped round her knees, looked down at the water. She wanted friends, and pretty clothes. She wanted laughter, and conversation. She wanted to be accepted at school, but never would be while she was dressed like an oddity. If only she had been born with blue eyes and blonde curly hair, and was tall and slim, with a figure like Miss McDonald, whom Kate thought one of the most beautiful women she had ever seen. Nearly as beautiful as her mother had been.

She wriggled inside her jeans. They were made of scratchy cotton that teased at her skin. When she was eight years old her mother had made her a party dress of pale blue material, embroidered with tiny white flowers. It had a flounced skirt and a big sash, and a little frill at the neck and more frills at the edge of the sleeves. She had loved it, and felt elegant and grown-up in it, had been bitterly unhappy when she had grown out of it. She couldn't remember the parties. She had never forgotten the dress.

No use daydreaming, Kate McKendrick, she told herself aloud, just to convince herself that she actually could speak. She went indoors and made a thick sandwich of bread and cheese and pickle, and took it up on the hill to eat. There were butterflies dancing on the heather, and a bee busy gathering pollen from the patches of bright flowers. The sea, for once calm, whispered softly at the edge of the loch, and the tangle of weed was bright in the unusually warm sun.

Kate sat on a rock and looked down at the spread of blue water, framed by hills that were misty and blue in the distance. Waves broke near the shore on a rocky island, and here, she was sure, the seals basked when the sun was hot. Perhaps her father would buy her some binoculars for her birthday.

She glanced down at the rock between her feet. There were blood marks, little scattered drops, bright red and fresh. Something had been hurt.

Kate was afraid again. Suppose the man who had been shooting was out there still and shot at her? Suppose it was her father that was injured? She had to know. She swallowed the last of her sandwich and began to follow the trail, up the hill, among the new-leafed trees that rustled and whispered in the wind.

The hunter had seen a flash of fur in the grass and thought there was a rabbit. The little cat had been hunting. He was on his way home, having eaten a couple of mice. The shot grazed his shoulder. Fear made him freeze. The man, tramping heavily down the hillside, could not find his victim, and thought he had missed.

The cat, terrified by noise and the wicked pain, lay still. The wound was not deep. A gouge in the fur, enough skin removed to bleed, but the nerve endings on the surface burned. He lay motionless, hiding himself from danger.

Kate, coming slowly up the hill, following the blood trail, saw him crouching deep in the heather, his terrified eyes staring straight into hers. She saw the long wound, and did not know what to do.

He was such a beautiful creature. His dense fur was tabby marked, his muzzle and a tiny triangle of shirtfront were white. The long thick whiskers were also white. Black tiger stripes on head and body and a thick tail, though not so bushy as she had expected. Perhaps he wasn't a true wild cat but part tame cat, as he reminded her of the school's big tabby Tammas.

He was bigger than Tammas, and his green eyes, which stared in fear into hers, were rimmed with black. Fur bushed inside his big ears. The striped fur on his shoulder was marred with blood, but it was already clotting and the wound perhaps was not too deep. He nerved himself and stood, fur fluffed, eyes wild with hate, and spat at her, hissing his horror of mankind, and then fled, leaving Kate watching him, longing to help him, to tame him, to feed him.

He was so handsome, but he was as wild as the eagle, and would be as difficult to tame. He did not trust humans and fear bushed his fur until he was a giant cat. He paused and turned, poised as if about to pounce, staring at the girl. He associated her with his pain. For a moment Kate thought he was going to spring at her.

Then he was gone, moving fast, only the blood drops to show he had ever been there at all.

Kate walked slowly back to the cottage. Clouds hid the sun, and a thin rain drenched the ground, and the wind, tormenting the sea, hissed through the leaves, sounding like a spitting cat.

She went in and lit the fire and sat on the floor, her head on her knees, watching the flames dance among the logs. Little bright flames that teased and changed colour, and grew and died away. Flames in which a wounded cat crept among the rocks to hide, flames that lit the room, and then faded, until Kate knew nothing more, and lay on the rug, curled up, as she had curled when she was a small girl, and slept, exhausted by the terrors of the day.

Gavin, coming in, unheard by his daughter, looked down at her, and was reminded of the baby girl who had crept into his arms each evening, and asked, "Had a busy day, daddy?" mimicking her mother.

He put down his filming apparatus and went out into the kitchen and began to prepare their meal, wondering desolately what was to become of them both.

Outside in the dark the cat tried to lick his wound, and far above him the eagles guarded their remaining youngster. One had gone, as Gavin had feared, but he did not see its fall, nor find its body. He only knew that one baby eagle remained.

The wind murmured round the cottage,

and whined under the eaves, and as it strengthened the remorseless sea crashed against the rocks, and Gavin felt as if all of nature conspired against him and mocked him.

5

HIGH on the hill the eagles brooded over their surviving youngster. The enormous beak was always open, the baby screaming for food. The parents hunted endlessly. Gavin, oversleeping, exhausted by his worries, was late at the site. He looked down, focusing the camera, seeing the hideous eaglet, beak wide open, peering from under the parent bird's vast bulk. No one would imagine that this screaming featherless mite would grow into such a magnificent bird.

If only they could rear this eaglet. The last two years had been barren. Someone had stolen the eggs the first time, and the second year they had lain unhatched, and, when taken by the temporary warden and broken, found to be poisoned by pesticides.

So many birds were dying out, their eggs contaminated by man's ruthless means of ensuring his food supply was safe from insects.

Far down the hill, hidden from her father among the low growing trees, newly planted only a couple of years before by the Forestry Commission, Kate crouched, watching the eyrie. The little white clouds sailed over a sky bluer than any she had seen, a brilliance of colour that exalted her spirits. It was impossible to be miserable on such a bright day.

Below her the sea, still wind-tossed, crashed against rocks, and the white spray plumed high, sparkling in the sunshine. The tide was receding, and the brilliant orange seawrack lay at its edge, lifting and shifting with each wave.

There was a movement on the beach. The cat was hunting at the edge of the tide. His shoulder burned fiercely, each step pulling at the ripped edges of the skin. He was thirsty, and stopped to lap at the water of a little burn that trickled down the cliff and fed into the loch.

He knew that the tide left fish behind, and the hunting was easy. He brooded over a rock pool, watching the flash and flirt of burnished fins as a tiny fish darted under the overhang and out into the sunlight again. His paw swept down, claws anchoring the small body against the shingly bottom, only a few inches down.

It was a very small mouthful, and with it came thirst again. He limped wearily back to the burn and drank, and then, aware now more of pain than hunger, stretched himself along a craggy shelf, basking in the sunshine. His green slant eyes half closed, he watched the wheeling gulls, and eased his pain-torn body into comfort.

Kate had seen him hunting by the pool, had seen him limp towards the burn, and now saw him stretched along the rocky shelf. She knew that he was hurt and the injury appeared worse than it had the day before, when the small blood spots had made her think this was only a glancing graze.

But even a graze could fester, though would it infect so fast?

She slipped through the trees to the edge of the cliff, and looked for a way down to the beach that wasn't too dangerous.

And that wouldn't alert the cat, and

send him diving for cover.

Kate's ready imagination came to her rescue. She was a spy, seeking information from the enemy, behind the enemy's line. She had to stalk silently. She must not be seen or she would be shot. Move slowly, foot by careful foot. Into a gully, which the sun's absence made dark and shivery and a little frightening. Beyond her, bright light teased against the sea holly and thrift, but here nothing grew, and the rockface was damp from the trickling water that seeped from the ground above.

She was Alice, going down the deep hole. Down, down, down, said Alice. Below her the walrus and the carpenter sang their song; below her was mystery and excitement. Below her was a wild cat that was dying from his wounds. She would tame him, so that he would follow her like a dog. She would sing to him, as the old people sang to the seals to bring them to the shore.

Perhaps there would be seals down there too, seals she could tame, so that one day she would write a book about all the wild beasts that had followed her. Orpheus and his lute . . . she had forgotten the words. He made the beasts and the trees bow to his music. That wasn't right.

Her foot slipped and there was the slithering unnerving tumble and rattle of a small pebble hitting the cliff and bouncing off, down towards the beach, down towards the wild cat that had lifted its head and for a moment seemed to stare right into her eyes with his own arrogant look.

Kate froze against the rock, stories forgotten, looking down, willing him to relax, to stay there. She could creep to within feet of him. She had food in her pocket. A sandwich she had made for her lunch. If he took it and ate it her scent would be on it. He would associate her smell with food smell and perhaps if she fed him daily he would accept her.

A gull wheeled as if to look at her, curious, and then soared up against the sky, his wings momentarily blotting out the sun. High in the air above another bird flew, and its huge shadow drifted over the gully, spreading against the rock.

The cat was aware of the shadow as it fled across him, chilling the air and hiding the sun. He glanced up, saw the eagle, and knew danger. He was vulnerable. His shoulder hurt and he was weakened by the wound. He dared not fight.

He vanished, down the edge of the rock, along a crack that Kate had not seen, and into a small cave, away from the great bird that threatened him.

Kate did not see him go. One moment he was there, and the next, was gone. She did not see how she could have missed the movement. She climbed down, and stood on the empty beach, her feet ankle deep in bright orange weed, the sun gilding her dark hair.

There were pools along the shore. A glint of a fin, and a flash of silver as a blenny darted into the sunlight and back into the shadow. Tiny transparent shrimps flirted through the water.

Beyond her, a gull paraded, his beak stabbing into the seaweed, in search of food. His bright beady eyes looked at her, and ignored her. She sat so still that he did not feel threatened.

Her hands stroked the cold stone. Tiny insects ran busily, darting on unimaginable affairs.

The cat had lain on this rock. There was no trace of him, and reassuringly, no bloodstains, which meant the wound at least was healing. Not a single hair.

Beyond her, there was a spit of damp sand, and there, in front of the darkness in the cliff, were two paw prints.

He was in the cave.

Kate took the food from her pocket and unwrapped it. There was a bread roll, buttered, with a thick hunk of meat cut from the joint they had had on Sunday. Gavin found it easier to buy a big lump of meat and cook it at the weekend, and then have it to cut cold for the next five days.

With frozen vegetables, or sauté potatoes, or a salad, it made catering quick and easy for both of them.

Kate broke the bread into small pieces. The meat was tough and she had to tear at it with her teeth. She scattered meat and bread at the mouth of the cave, throwing it from the side, so that she could not be seen, though, as the wind blew across her, she was sure the cat would scent her.

If only he were hungry enough not to worry about the human taint.

If only the circling gulls were not so fast that they took the food before she had gone. She knew better than to stay. She walked noisily across the shingle and then began to climb the cliff again.

This time she climbed in sunlight, and took shelter behind a little bush that grew, improbably, at right angles to the rock, its roots embedded into a small pocket of dark soil.

A seagull swooped and took one of the pieces of bread.

The wind blew the scent of the food to the cat, and with it an alien scent that worried him. Hunger triumphed, and he walked out into the glare, spitting furiously at another gull that hovered, ready to snatch. The bird knew better than to argue with a wild cat. That battle he was sure to lose.

The wide wings almost brushed Kate's face as the bird soared.

Meat!

The cat forgot his pain and began to

eat, following the trail that Kate had laid. Bread, tasting of meat; and good roast pork, making his salivary juices work overtime. By the time he had finished he had accepted the alien scent, and lay again on the rock in the sun, watchful, wary, eyes half closed, savouring the life-giving heat on his aching shoulder.

Kate climbed back to the clifftop and lay watching him. The sun burnished his fur, and she could see the long slash of darkness where the shot had grazed his skin. He moved several times, as if easing himself to find a more comfortable position.

Above him the gulls wheeled and soared, their plaintive cries sorrowing the air. Chin on paws, he ignored them.

The sea crept out, inch by inch, the waves' fury dying as the tide receded. Little foam-flecked ripples inched across the sand. When the tide was low, and grey clouds had begun to build on the horizon and mask the sun, the cat stood and stretched his hind legs. He licked frantically towards his sore shoulder. He licked first one front paw and then the other, moving the left one slowly, and washed the food from his fur and whiskers.

A sick cat never washes. So he wasn't too sick. Her mother had said that long ago. They had a white cat then. She had named him Blackie and her parents had laughed together at the name, but allowed her to keep it, as the farmer had let her name his bull calf Macaroni. Mac for short. They had holidayed there on a Cornish farm long ago when she was very small and so young, only four years old and thought she was a grown up girl as they had a little baby, not yet a year old.

Now she felt a hundred years old. Aged and responsible, not only for her father but for this cat. He reminded her of Blackie. Reminded her not in appearance, but in his cat ways. In the way he moved and the licking front paws that swept across his face. In the lifted hind paw, thrust stiffly over his shoulder, so undignified as he licked beneath his tail to clean himself.

In the way he walked.

Blackie had died on the road a year before her mother had died. They had buried him in the garden and she put flowers on his grave and cried for him. There was no one this year to put flowers on her mother's grave. Would she mind? Did she know? Was she there, somewhere, watching over them and sad for them, guarding them, like an angel, from harm?

Kate rolled over and looked at the sky. The sun had vanished, leaving only a toss of rolling grey clouds. Warmth was a memory. A chill wind shivered the grass. Below her the tide had turned and a grey sea teased a drab beach, empty of life.

Above her, a rabbit fled across the moor, pursued by a giant shape that dropped from the sky. A scream tore the air, and the eagle lifted purposefully, winging back to his mate and the demanding gaping mouth that now dominated both their lives. He brought not only food to the nest but fresh green branches.

Gavin, filming, safely hidden in his hide, was so absorbed that he did not stop until darkness dropped over the hills. Kate had prepared the evening meal with care. Cold meat and a tossed salad,

95

made as her mother used to make it, with a home-made dressing rich in garlic that her father loved. Soft potatoes cooked to perfection, golden brown.

She had waited for him, and finally, when it was almost dark, had eaten alone, and gone to her room to read. Sleep overtook her, long before he came, and she dreamed of a cat that played and pounced on a feather and was now white and now tiger-striped with white chest and white paws and glowing green eyes that mocked her with their supercilious stare.

She woke to hear her father's key in the door. Stiffly, she stood up, and then went down the narrow winding stairs to the big room where the log fire had burned low, and only glowing ashes reminded her of the blaze she had left.

She removed the guard and blew the ash to flame and added more logs, and watched them catch and brighten.

"I waited and waited and you never came," she said, bringing her father's plate and putting it in front of him. "The potatoes will be horrible. I'll cook some more."

He seemed to have nothing to say to her. His mind was filled with the eagles, and the film he had shot that day. Film that would make his work known; film that might gain an award, and ensure that he never lacked work again and could keep himself and his daughter without the fear of unemployment. How could he talk of such things to little Kate, still only a baby in years?

Kate wanted to tell him about the wild cat. Perhaps he could take pictures of it. Perhaps he could make a film of it. But he wouldn't want to do that. His interest had always been in birds, and never in animals.

If only she had a little video camera and could make her own film. And then, when it was complete, show it to her father and earn his praise. He never did praise her now; he never even kissed her goodnight. He never touched her. He behaved as if she were infectious, keeping a distance, drawing back if she moved towards him, longing for the feel of his arms strong around her, for the touch of his chin against her head, for the old familiar "Goodnight, princess," of her young days. Perhaps he hated her for being alive when her mother was dead.

She was growing up now. Maybe that was what growing up meant. Being alone, no one to share thoughts with, no one to laugh with, no one to tell the little happenings of the day.

"I saw a tiny crab, no bigger than my fingernail, on the beach. It stood on tiptoe and waved its nippers at me." He'd think her daft if she said that. But it had been funny.

Her mother would have understood.

Kate suddenly hated the cottage; hated the loneliness. It wasn't too bad in term time except the other children hadn't accepted her. But she could talk to her teacher. Miss McDonald did laugh. Her eyes were green, like the wild cat's eyes, but not insolent or arrogant. They were kind eyes.

Maybe when Kate went back to school she could write about the crab on the beach and the little waves that tickled the sand, and the huge rollers that tortured the cliffs and the wind that savaged the trees and screamed round the cottage on wild nights like a beast in pain.

Maybe she could write it now; put down her thoughts on paper, talk to her notebook; and maybe when she was older someone would publish it as they had published little Daisy's story . . . but that was funny and what Kate felt wasn't at all funny.

The potatoes were not as well cooked as before. Maybe the cat would eat those, even if they were not meat. He would be finding it difficult to hunt with a lame leg; perhaps he couldn't run fast, or pounce, and if Kate didn't feed him he would starve to death.

Gavin took the food and ate it as if Kate were not there at all. He was still in his hide, his mind filled with the excitement of watching the great birds, the glow of the sun on their feathers, the little eagle's weird cries and the gaping beak.

If only he dared tell Kate, but it would be too much to expect her to keep it secret and it only needed the wrong ears to hear and the nest would be raided. Maybe the birds would be shot. Nobody walked the hills here. Only the postman came and he would have no eyes for the birds above him.

If only he had someone to talk to. He could have confided in his wife; she never told any secrets and she shared his passion for filming and for birds. They had been more than a married couple; they had been a working team. What had he done to offend the gods that they took her from him?

Kate, lying on the shaggy sheepskin hearthrug, looked into the flames and saw herself long ago, watching the dancing plumes of yellow and red and green, and listening to her mother reading aloud. They had both loved poetry and though sometimes the poems they read were too old for a child, Kate had loved the wonder of the words, the lilt and the rhyme and the rhythm.

Outside the wind was worsening, tossing through the small trees, its voice raging. Soon it would riot even more, scudding along the shore, so that the waves broke with a crash and thunder and a deep sucking sound as they drew back, only to hurl themselves against the rocks again.

Kate could not remember any poems about gales and rough seas, and the toss and bluster and wild fury of the night outside. The wind seemed to blow so often here, screaming round the corners of the little cottage, shaking the doors and windows so that they rattled as if some alien spirit were trying desperately to get in.

There was one poem:

Whenever the moon and stars are
   set,
Whenever the wind is high,
All night long in the dark and wet,
A man goes galloping by.

She knew the words weren't right. She would have to find the poem, but did not know where to look. All her mother's books were still packed in a crate in the empty bedroom upstairs. One day, she would take them out, but not yet.

Her mother had recited that poem to her so often when she was a small girl. She had loved it, and repeated it to herself in bed when the wind was fierce. She had never liked wind. The gales seemed far worse here, the wind noise augmented by the sea's relentless sound. Dreamily, Kate said the first verse of the poem aloud, in the sort of voice her mother had used.

Gavin, hearing her, was shocked back to happier days, and for a moment he shared Kate's vision, and saw his wife, her eyes laughing, the light shining on her hair, so like Kate's hair, and heard her soft voice reading the words aloud. He couldn't bear the memory. The pain of his wife's sudden death was re-awakened, fresh as yesterday, as if the healing time had never been.

He crashed his fist down on the table and shouted at Kate.

"Don't you ever do that again. Do you hear?"

He couldn't bear it. He couldn't bear to remember. Kate, terrified by his violence, startled out of her reverie, jumped to her feet, tears pouring down her cheeks.

"I hate you," she shouted. "I hate you. Why did Mummy have to die?"

The door slammed behind her.

Gavin, shocked by her reaction, cursed his own, and pushed away his plate, all appetite gone. He had no idea what to do. He wanted to follow Kate to her room, to cradle her in his arms, to whisper into her hair. But that could be misconstrued if she ever told anyone, and children did talk.

Damn the world he lived in. He hated it. He made up the fire and sat by the bright burning logs until the moon crept up the stormy sky and set again, and the first hesitant light coloured the silent room, and the fire was as exhausted as the feelings that had shaken him all night. Then he fell asleep.

Kate slept on, her face stained by dried tears.

Outside her window the injured cat crouched, brought by the memory of her scent to hope for food. His shoulder hurt and flared with the pain of an injury now turning septic, throbbing and aching, and hindering his hunting.

Gavin, defeated by his thoughts, slept in his chair, and did not wake until the sun shone across his face. Brightness had returned. The sky was brilliant blue, without a cloud in sight, and the wind was a sighing ripple across the surface of silken sea, and the trees moved softly, as if easing their own bruised branches.

Gavin made tea for both of them and took a cup up to Kate's bedside. He looked down at her, his eyes brooding, hating himself.

"Kate," he said softly.

She woke, uncurling, and stretching like a kitten, and yawned. She stared up at him, her eyes wide, her expression unfathomable.

"I'm sorry," he said.

There was no forgiveness in his daughter's face. She turned her back on him, and stared at the wall. Her rebuff was like a blow. He put the cup down and went out of the room. Kate did not move until she heard his footsteps die away outside as he went back to the eyrie to continue filming.

One day, she would run away.

6

SHEINA McDONALD was haunted. The haunting annoyed her as she tried, very hard, not to get involved with her pupils. But everywhere she went she saw Kate's white face and tormented eyes. The expression in the child's eyes bothered Sheina immensely. It came between her and her work, and made her absent-minded. There was something very wrong.

"You haven't heard a word I said." Bruce Wilson, who was in charge of the school Art Department, had been trying to rouse interest in a competition for the children. A painting of an animal, with a prize for the best. He looked at Sheina, an exasperated expression in his eyes.

"Are you in love or something?"

The idle question irritated Sheina. The staffroom theory was that Bruce was wedded to his art and had never known affection for any human. He spent every hour that he was free painting the wild moors and the high hills and the stormy waters of the hidden lochs.

"Bruce, do you teach the little McKendrick girl?"

"Kate? Yes. Why?"

"What does she draw? Can she draw?"

"She can draw. She has an eye for colour and shape, and she's interested. Mostly, she draws cats if left to herself."

Cats. Why cats? Had the child a cat?

"Does she talk to you?"

"That one doesn't talk to anyone. Yes, and no, is about all I ever have from her. She's a dreamer. Leave it, Sheina. There's nothing we can do. The child's all right. An oddity, perhaps, but that's all. She's lost her mother recently and not settled in the school. Give it time."

"She'd be less of an oddity if that wretched father of hers had any idea about clothes. She looks like Orphan Annie and the other children tease her. It isn't fair."

"And when were children ever fair to one another? Or kind? We can teach them, we can try to influence them, but we can never get the pack instinct out of them. They herd together against the newcomer, and it takes a lot of time to break that down. Adults do it too. Try joining a new club. How many people make you welcome?"

"There's more to it than that."

"Och, woman," Bruce hit the table with his fist. "When you get an idea in your head you're as bad as a dog gnawing away at a bone. Worry and nag it. Maybe not, though, as the bone gets smaller and your ideas grow and balloon out of proportion. Don't worry so much about the lass. She just needs time."

Men were about the most unperceptive of all creatures, Sheina thought in fury, as she slammed out of the room. And Bruce was one of the most exasperating and if there was anything she hated it was being called 'woman' as if she had no name to her.

She had no real women friends at all; and no men to whom she could talk. It was Friday morning. Sheina walked into a babel of noise that fluttered and died as the children saw her expression. This was no morning for skylarking. Miss McDonald was in one of her moods.

There was an uneasy atmosphere in

the class, even when the children had settled. Stray giggles and sniggers, and eyes that met and rolled skywards. A nudged elbow, and a dip of the head, and that Sheina caught. Following the direction of the interested eyes, she saw that Kate, as so often, was the focus of their attention.

The child sat still, huddled into herself, as if enduring some inner torment. Her eyes were suspiciously puffy, as if she had been crying. Her clothes were even odder than usual, and it was this that was triggering the children, who stared at her with wild delight. Her outfit was astonishing, even for Kate.

Her father had forgotten to do any washing, and Kate hadn't thought of it. There was nothing clean that she could find of her own. She was wearing a skirt that had been her mother's, overlooked among Kate's belongings when they had packed. A neighbour helping them had thought it might come in useful for the child one day. She was growing fast. It was made of grey corduroy, pinned at the waist as it was too big. On top of that Kate had put a sweatshirt of her father's that had been given to him by a friend long ago and he had hated. It was black and covered with little red fish. Her socks were brown and her shoes were old trainers, that she had fished out of a cupboard as those she usually wore were too tight for her.

They had packed very oddly when they left home, Kate had thought that morning, burrowing in the chests of drawers in frantic desperation for clean clothes to wear.

It was a chilly morning with a bite in the air and her jacket was so tight that it strained across new developing breasts of which she was horribly conscious. She had crowned her outfit with one of her father's old anoraks. It was a shabby camouflage jacket, in shades of green and brown and most unsuitable wear for a child at school.

Sheina could not concentrate on her lesson. She was too aware of Kate, sitting in dumb misery, and the sniggers of the other children, and exchanged looks and rolled eyes. There was a parents' evening next week, and Sheina would have a word with the man. Anger rode her every time she looked at Kate.

They were studying English, but the lesson was going badly. The children were restive, and much of that, Sheina knew, was due to her own mood. They would take a break and she would read them some poetry. That, next to music, soothed the savage breasts. Too aware of Kate, she had almost identified with her and hated the other children, wanting to shake them, to shout at them. Don't be so cruel. Can't you see she's unhappy? Why can't you accept her, make her feel wanted, leave her in peace from your constant teasing? Why did they have to be such little beasts?

The law of the jungle, killing the outsider. They didn't kill. Perhaps death was kinder. Did animals suffer when they were rejected by the pack?

Sheina tried to calm her racing thoughts which were doing no one any good. She glanced across the room and caught Kate's eyes. Dear heaven. There was something appallingly wrong with that child.

Outside the classroom was a grey overcast sky, and the wind keening through the trees. Children were always worse on a windy day.

The school was within sight of the loch. The waves crashed and broke in flurries of spray, and sped skyward in foamy fountains that caught the light. Kate looked out of the window, longing to be alone on the beach, to stand and watch the wild combers clawing at the rocks.

She wouldn't think of her father, or his anger. She would forget what had happened and think about the cat. His shoulder was badly injured. He might die. He mustn't die. He was so beautiful. If only she could save him; could tame him, and have his company. Maybe she could stand living with her father then.

Rain drummed on the window, flung by the wind. Sheina felt the class stirring as if they were being wound up by some unseen hand. Nothing would settle them.

She wanted a poem about wind, but they were hard to find.

And then she remembered one of her own childhood favourites.

"Come on, children," she said. "Put

your books away and I'll read to you.
Only you must sit still. I'm going to
read you a poem about the wind. When
I've read it I want you to draw a picture;
something that the poem reminds you of.
Now listen hard."

Kate loved poetry. She brought her
mind back to her scratched desk and
shut the book that was in front of her,
preparing herself for a feast.

She listened in disbelief and growing
horror.

"Whenever the moon and stars are
    set,
Whenever the wind is high,
All night long in the dark and wet,
A man goes riding by.
Late in the night when the fires
    are out,
Why does he gallop and gallop
    about?"

Too late Sheina saw Kate's white face
and appalled eyes. Too late to stop the
child racing from her desk and through
the door, slamming it behind her. Too
late to catch her as she sped down the

corridor and out into the playground, and through the school gate, away from the words that mocked her and taunted her and reminded her of the past. And of her father yelling at her when she recited them dreamily only the night before.

She couldn't bear it any more.

She would go away and never come back. She would hide on the hills with only the cat for company. She would feed on wild berries and roots, and catch fish from the sea, and live by herself in a cave, without people who hurt her all the time.

She ran until her breath came fast and her chest ached. She slowed to a walk, ignoring the rain that drenched down from the hills, soaking her. Snatches of other poems her mother had read to her slipped through her mind.

When I stood lone on the height my
     sorrow did speak,
As I went down the hill, I cried and
     I cried,
The soft little hands of the rain
     stroking my cheek,
The kind little feet of the rain ran
     by my side.

"I always read that when I'm sad," her mother had said.

Kate had read it again and again when her mother died. Somehow the words of the poem made it easier.

When I went to thy grave, broken
  with tears,
When I crouched down in the grass,
  dumb in despair . . .

She couldn't even visit her mother's grave. There was nothing of her left here, except memory. Maybe she would go home and get some food and get her poetry book, and then leave for good. Her father would be glad, he wouldn't miss her. He was never there.

She walked until the school was remote, left behind her, no longer important. She walked with the wind on her face and the thin rain stinging her. She walked, her feet hurting, her skirt dragging, for over three hours, until she reached the hill of the eagles and dropped into the heather, and lay there, sobbing in great gasps that she couldn't control.

Above her, in his hide near the eyrie,

114

Gavin filmed, his mind only half on his work. He shouldn't have shouted at Kate, but she had hurt him so much. Brought back the past with such vividness that his wife might have been sitting there beside him, reciting to them both.

Memory was a traitor, triggering pain. The child had no idea her voice was so like her mother's, nor till that moment had he. He felt as if a new wound had opened and he was raw with misery. He knew he had hurt Kate, possibly beyond repair. He had lost her trust.

In the school, Sheina was almost sick with anxiety. No child had ever run out of her class like that before, and she had seen Kate's face for a brief appalled moment. The child looked as if she were being chased by demons. Sheina raced after her, but the child had vanished, and she had no idea which direction she had taken.

As soon as the lesson ended she went to the headmaster. He was a small man, barely five feet three inches tall, but nobody ever noticed his lack of size. He dominated every room when he walked in. Fierce blue eyes stared at Sheina, hating every word she spoke. Rough impatient hands tangled his neat grey hair, as he listened, the only sign he ever gave of being disturbed by anything he heard. His fingers pushed through the curls again and again as the story unfolded. He despaired of all children.

Why had he ever taken on this job? His frowning gaze daunted Sheina but she struggled on. He hated any disruption in his school. He should have been in the Army, Sheina thought, with all of us parading for him and nothing ever allowed to go wrong. He can never cope with this sort of emergency.

She tried to remember being thirteen and came up with a memory she would rather have forgotten. She was to play in the school tennis team for under fourteens and on the morning of the match had fallen and broken her wrist. She couldn't play in the team. It was a bitter disappointment. She had been so excited, which was how she came to fall, rushing to school, eager to get there fast. She had tripped in the playground before morning lessons. It had seemed like the end of the world and she had sobbed inconsolably, not for the pain, but for the missed chance. She might never be chosen for the team again. Her wrist might be too weak to play again as it was her right wrist.

Her misery had been out of all proportion to the event, and her parents and teachers and even the doctor had been impatient with her, unable to understand her grief or what was driving her to such extremes.

She was sure there was something far more wrong than that with Kate's world.

"I want to talk to her father. I want to find the child. She could harm herself; or be harmed. God knows where she's gone. Or what made her act like that."

Grant Hamilton was within a year of retirement. He was tired of his role in life; longing for peaceful days without any problems and the chance to go fishing whenever he chose. He thought of a quiet burn, shadowed by overhanging trees, of the bright water rippling over rounded boulders, of the fish rising, and the sun shining on the hills but not on the stream. He could almost feel the rod in his hands, hear the swish as he flung the fly, see it settle, so gently, and savour the sudden thrill of the fish biting, and the dancing line.

"It doesna do to interfere." His accent was always more noticeable when he was upset and he was very upset now, not knowing what to advise, not having any past experience to draw on. He had noticed the child and her odd clothes, and been irritated by her silences. She behaved as if he were an ogre, whispering when he spoke to her, as if terrified of him. He did not realise that Kate was very much in awe of him and overcome with extreme shyness when he spoke to her.

"Maybe you should see the father at the end of the day. He is unlikely to be at his home now, and we do not know where he works."

"The village mystery man," Sheina said, irritation in her voice. Everyone speculated about the father and daughter, out there on the lonely moors.

"The child has probably gone home. I do not see how a poem could have produced such an effect." There was more than annoyance in the headmaster's voice. There was sudden worry. Suppose she had been taken ill, and was lying somewhere on the hills, in pain with a burst appendix? The school could be sued.

And if that came first into his thoughts it was high time he retired, he thought sourly, and rubbed his hands again through the thick thatch of hair, so that Sheina nearly giggled as he reminded her of a startled owl.

The day dragged to its weary end. Sheina, at the end of it, putting on her outdoor clothes, could not remember any of the lessons she had given. The worry about Kate had flared into an overwhelming anxiety. Supposing someone had offered the child a lift and harmed her? Supposing she had run to the beach which she loved so much and fallen on the rocks and was lying injured?

And where in the world did one start to look?

First find out if the child had gone home. Maybe she was safely there all the time.

The rain had eased, but the wind still blustered noisily, accompanying Sheina along the narrow twisting road, and up the hill. The wind noise irritated her. The road ended in little more than a track, and she stopped the car, and walked up to the cottage. Blind windows stared at her impassively. She knocked but no one came.

She turned and stared out at the rain-sodden moors, at the grey impassive sky, at the waves breaking over the rocks. It was a wild place and a lonely place and no place to bring a sensitive child. What company had she here?

And where in the world was the man who had fathered her, and then apparently abdicated all responsibility for her?

The rain had driven Gavin from his hide. No point in filming today. Mist clouded the camera lens and the birds were hidden from him. He came down the hill slowly, wondering what he was going to say to Kate, wondering how to bridge the rift that had opened between them.

He had been an only child, with a

doting mother who had given him little experience of girls. His father, a shy man, had had little time to spend with his son, and it never occurred to Gavin that men did give up time to children.

His work had often taken him away from home, filming in foreign lands, and Kate had been an adored child, but, he now realised, a child he barely knew. In the time since his wife had died, they had seemed to drift further apart. He had been lost in his own grief.

The child must miss her mother terribly, he thought, anger at his own folly needling him, so that he quickened his pace. She would be home and he would make it up to her. Somehow. He had no idea how.

He turned the corner of the cottage, and was startled to discover a strange woman standing there, staring at him. Sheina's eyes were bright with worry and with anger. She saw a tall dark man, his hair streaked with grey, his face drawn and tired. The child was not like him; she must favour her mother.

"Yes?" he said, wishing this stranger away, wanting to get into the house and find Kate and hold her and tell her how precious she was to him.

"I'm Sheina McDonald. Kate's form mistress. Kate ran away from school this morning. I came to see if she were home. She isn't."

Gavin stared at her. The mist that had been hiding the tops had drifted down the hillside, and was swirling around them, so that the loch was already hidden. The damp greyness that surrounded them reflected his plunging spirits.

He glanced at his watch.

It was well after five o'clock and Kate should have been home more than an hour ago.

Sheina had been intending to speak her mind, to upbraid this careless father who didn't care about his daughter at all. She knew, as she stood there, watching his stricken face, that she had read the scenario wrongly.

Gavin had thought there was nothing worse to bear than the problems he had already. Now he knew that was not true. He looked at the drifting mist. It was cold, and Kate was somewhere out there, alone.

"Where in the world is she?" he asked, despair in his voice. "And what on earth do we do? Where can we start to look?"

Sheina peered up the hill. Wisps of cloud drifted across her eyes and foiled her. They were isolated in a wreathing cocoon, and all sounds were muted. Where would the child go? Suppose she had fallen and were lying with a broken leg, or worse, were lying dead?

"You'd better get in my car," she said, practicality reasserting itself. "We must get out a search party. All the village will help."

Gavin had lost the ability to think for himself. He sat in the passenger seat, as they bumped along the illmade road, and tried to concentrate on eagles. He was too afraid to think of Kate.

He cursed the mist that defeated vision. It might trap the child into danger. He should never have brought her to this desolate place.

7

KATE sobbed until she was exhausted. She did not notice the rain, or feel the cold. She drifted into an uneasy doze. She woke, startled, as, far above her, an eagle screamed. She shivered. Her skirt was clammy against her body, but the thick anorak was waterproof and her top half at least was dry.

The mist had crept around her, unseen. She stared out into wreathing coils of vapour, trying to get her bearings. She had not noticed where she was walking, and had no idea of landmarks.

Behind her the rock was hard and wet. She was cramped, and stiff, and very cold, and her eyes were gritty and sore. She was hungry.

But at least she had had the sense to grab her anorak and her satchel, before she fled from the school.

She flexed her legs, stretching first one foot and then another, and then sat on a boulder and delved, bringing out her lunch pack. She tore at the bread. It was stale. They often forgot to buy new loaves. The meat was tough and overcooked, but the pickle she had lavished on it tasted good. She wished she had a hot drink. The little pack of orange juice would satisfy her thirst but wouldn't warm her. She would not eat all the food. Heaven alone knew when she might eat again.

She lifted the carton and broke the tiny metal circle with the straw, and drank.

It was no use running away. Where could she go? Where could she hide? How could she live?

In books there were wonderful children who built themselves shelters and caught fish and lived on berries. They must always run away in autumn. There were no berries now. Or they found shelter with unlikely people, themselves isolated, or perhaps they were tramps.

Today anyone she approached would at once ring the police if a child turned up on their doorstep asking for shelter. Here, where there were so few people, everybody would know her. She couldn't pretend to be the child of a summer visitor. It wasn't time for those yet, anyway.

There would be television appeals. Her father would surely go to the police, not just leave her? Maybe he wouldn't care. Just be glad he no longer had her to hinder him and tell everyone she had gone back to live with relatives. Nobody knew they hadn't any.

Her father must care? She hugged the long anorak round her, conjuring up a vision of him begging desperately for her to return. Or putting an appeal in the personal column of a newspaper. 'Kate. All is forgiven. Come home. I love you. Dad.'

She might die here in the mist. Die of exposure. People did die on the moors, even in high summer. Would he be sorry? Hypothermia. That was the word and she was sure she was suffering from it already. She was so cold.

Her father had warned her often enough about the dangers of the hills when the white mist drifted and the land and loch alike were hidden. Too easy to drop into a rift, or over the

126

edges and drown in the tumbling waves. Drown like Ophelia only she hadn't long blonde hair to drift like weed on the water. Was Ophelia blonde? What silly things she seemed to be thinking, but if she thought about Ophelia she didn't think about her father, or the cold.

She shivered.

Her father had a book of poems about the Scottish hills, which Kate read, loving only those with a lilt and a rhythm.

Two lines came into her head.

The mountain where I danced on
    moonlit stones
Has killed children.

She was on the edge of a mountain and high above her was the eagle's nest and her father's hide. The mist was thicker, choking her. If only the wind would rise and blow it away. If it didn't blow away this mountain might well kill a child. Would she be with her mother then?

She didn't want to die of cold, or of tumbling down the treacherous slippery rocks to shatter on the boulder-strewn beach. The healing tangle. She could smell the rotting seaweed on the air. She thought she could hear the soft slither and suck of the waves against the beach. She must be very near the sea.

How near? How high?

It was very still and the stillness was terrifying. There were tiny flowers at her feet; yellow, with a scarlet centre, looking like a red eye. Fairy flowers, growing among the unkind stones.

Behind her was the muted grumble of a waterfall, far enough away to be a reassuring sound. Kate tried to remember how far it was from her home. She ached for the cottage, and the dancing flames of the log fire, and her place on the hearthrug, lying there, propped on her elbows, dreaming stories that, one day, she would write.

If she lived to dance on the moonlit stones of the mountain and not to lie dead at its feet.

She had been stupid to run. So stupid. But she had not been able to bear those words, or the memory they evoked. The memory of her mother, sitting beside the fire, on the hearthrug, her arm round her small daughter, the deep voice soft, always with a murmur of laughter behind it.

Yesterday had been the anniversary of her mother's birthday, and her father hadn't even remembered. And there was no grave near to visit, to lavish with flowers, to salve the hurt that persisted and, after she had looked at the calendar, had grown so great that she thought she couldn't bear it.

Her father rarely talked to her. She was so lonely. There was another poem, that her mother had read to her once. So long ago. Soon after her grandfather had died.

They told me, Heraclitus, they told
    me you were dead,
They brought me bitter news to hear
    and bitter tears to shed.
I wept as I remembered how often
    you and I
Had tired the sun with talking till
    we sent him down the sky.

If only the wind would rise and blow the mist away. Her mother had loved poetry and Kate had kept all her books and brooded over them. So often when they were alone her mother read her favourites.

Kate, crouching in the mist, huddling into herself, trying to keep warm, had a sudden memory of one particularly awful day when everything had gone wrong at school. Her best friend had copied from Kate's arithmetic book. They had both had the same two wrong answers. Lynne, who was blonde with curly hair and enormous dark eyes that always looked so innocent, said that Kate had copied from her. Kate had been sent to the headmistress for cheating. That was the worst crime that anyone in their school could commit.

The headmistress was a terrifying woman, six feet tall with dark hair braided on top of her head, adding to her height. She always wore her gown, which swept out behind her when she strode round the school. Her eyes flashed with anger. Kate had added to her sin by lying. Own up and the punishment would be less.

Kate did not intend to own up to a crime she hadn't committed. She was to learn a psalm a day for the whole week and come and recite it each morning before prayers to the Head herself. Kate had not met unfairness before.

Nobody believed her, except her mother, who had experience of Lynne's duplicity when the child had come to tea. Kate had been hurt by betrayal, by knowing that her friend could never be trusted. And Lynne had laughed when Kate had railed at her.

"Everyone for herself in this world, my girl," she said, mockingly. Kate had not known that Lynne was quoting her father, who admired sharp business practices above everything else and who taught his children that all that mattered in life was to be one step ahead, never mind how you got there.

Kate had thought they were friends, and now she wondered what lay behind the watching eyes, what they said behind her back. She was branded before the whole class, unjustly, as a cheat.

"It isn't fair," she had shouted desperately, arriving home in a burst of stormy tears that could not at first be calmed. Her mother had toasted crumpets for her, a rare treat, comforting her as best she could and then begun to talk about life's problems, and how much worse they were when you grew up.

Kate, sure that adults had no problems and everything would be miraculously solved and fair and just when she was grown up, had listened in disbelief. She had been so young then, only eleven and in her first year at the senior school.

"I used to feel life was awful too," her mother said. "I wrote the most gloomy poetry, full of despair, especially when I was about sixteen and blighted in love. His name was Georgie Biggs and he had freckles and spots and my mother thought he was dreadful. He made me laugh. And then he took my best friend to the school dance."

Kate had never thought of her mother as being as young as sixteen and having boy friends who left her for somebody else. All those years before she was born when her parents were both living their own lives, growing up from babies too.

It was better to think back and remember than to contemplate the fall down the cliff, and the mist never clearing and herself dying of cold.

Her mother had been sitting in the big winged chair. She had been knitting. Kate could almost see the Fairisle pattern and the wool on the needles, and hear the soft voice.

Her mother's memory had been triggered by her daughter's misery.

She had gone on talking, dreamily, giving Kate time to recover herself.

"My favourite poem then was Mary Queen of Scots' lament. Now that poor woman had troubles! And she wrote, 'Worm in the heart and canker in the head, There is no peace for any but the dead.'" It wasn't a poem Kate wanted to remember. Her mother was dead. Was she at peace? And why was God so cruel? Her mother had never done anything wrong and yet had to die in a crash of metal sliding on an icy road. It wasn't fair.

Nor was it fair that her father didn't seem to realise Kate was growing up, was no longer a little girl who couldn't be trusted to talk sense, and who wanted only to live in her safe and sheltered world and play with her dolls.

She wished he would buy her some new clothes. Pretty clothes. Then perhaps the other children wouldn't laugh at her. There was a break in the mist and through it she saw the hillside plunging down, terrifyingly, to the loch far below. And then the mist returned and she crouched against the cliff, realising how near she was to a crashing fall that would land her, broken, on the beach.

She tried to think of happier times, but always they took her back to the days when her mother was alive. Until last night, the memory had been cherished. Now it was spoiled and again she heard her father's shout, saw his angry face, the fury in his eyes that had frightened her. But he had said he was sorry, this morning. Kate had a vision of his face then, white and worried, his eyes looking down at her, as if he were as bewildered as she felt. She had refused his offer of friendship, had turned away.

And now she might die for her stupidity. He had loved her mother too and known her for far longer than Kate had. She should have forgiven him. She should not have run out of school. God was making her pay for it, by bringing her into danger.

She dared not move far. She had to move. She was cold and cramped, and fear was growing so that it dried her mouth, and she could hear her thudding heart. She had to think. She was so cold. She dared only go upwards, clinging to the harsh surface of the crag. She had been on a tiny ledge, not more than a few feet wide, having lost her way over the moor as she ran. Not heeding. Not seeing, blinded by tears.

One step at a time, her hand against the sheltering rock, her foot feeling for hard ground. Then suddenly, her right hand felt nothing. The ground beneath her feet was covered with tiny pebbles. She could see them dimly through the swirling cloud. She had never seen anything so dense as that cloud.

How far could she see? A couple of feet, not more. There was a sound from the space beside her, and a movement. She leaned against the stone, her breath gasping, her heart racing. The mutter of the fall was nearer, filling the silence with noise. It was no longer friendly, but threatening.

That was not what she had heard.

Suppose some old tramp slept here in a cave? Or an outlaw, banned from the village, preying on women and little girls? It wasn't possible to grow up in the modern world without knowing the terrors that stalked the darkness, and preyed on the innocent and unwary.

A hand at her throat, dragging at her; a fierce face laughing at her, cold eyes staring at her. Kate crouched, as if that alone would hide her, and the sound came again. She could not identify it. It was an odd sound, a soft sound, an unnatural sound, magnified somehow by the mist, so that it echoed behind her. The pad pad pad of soft-shoe'd feet that came relentlessly on.

He was on her, almost touching her, and she was about to scream.

The scream died in her throat as the cat limped out of the cave. For a moment they stared at one another. Mist wreathed around him so that he was a ghost animal, a spectre raised from her imagination. But the green glare, so close to her, was real. She could see the dark slit down the centre of his slanting eyes, and the dark rims that outlined them.

White whiskers, black nose, and the small red mouth. He opened it in a faint mew, and white teeth glittered. She could see the red barred tongue. The wound on his shoulder was worse, a mass of festering flesh. He was so close she could have touched him.

They stared for a moment, face almost to face as Kate was still crouched low. Her fear died, but the cat lifted his lips in a silent snarl and backed away.

Kate forgot she was cold. There was a bar of chocolate as well as an apple and a bread roll filled with meat still in her satchel.

The cat could have the roll. She knelt. The cat watched her. His shoulder was a throb of needling pain, and he could only limp. The will to live was weakening in him. He had gone to shelter, recognising death without knowing what that was. It came nearer every hour. If he could not hunt he could not feed. And the wound would never heal without human help. He knew nothing of that.

He had lain for hours, licking at the water that formed in small pools on the ground. His last hunting foray had ended in despair as he pounced clumsily on a rabbit and fell sideways, with no hope of catching the animal that bounded swiftly to safety.

He was too weak to brave the steeply dropping hillside and hunt the tidal pools where fish might be easier prey.

It had taken him two hours to crawl back to the shelter of the little cave, out of the wind and the rain. There he lay and tried to lick at the knifing hurt, and slept and dreamed of being strong again.

He woke to a sound and a scent he knew. The girl had fed him before. She meant food. He watched suspiciously as she unfastened the buckles of her bag and rummaged inside it. He could smell the food which she held in her hand. Hunger was a raging ache.

Wildness gave way to weakness.

The mist encircled them, so that he had to come close to see her. He stared at her. His mouth watered. He craved for food.

He caught the meat smell and the hunger that had been tearing at him for three days overcame his last defences. He crept forwards. Kate broke the bread into pieces and threw them, one by one, towards him, making sure that each one was nearer to her.

He ate the fragments, crouching over them, watching her with a blazing stare. He had never been so close to a human before. She held out the pieces of meat. There were two of them, cut thick. She couldn't break them in her fingers. They were tough.

Memory triggered action. She tore at the meat with her teeth. The cat watched her, and she held out a small piece to him, in her hand.

Meat!

He snatched it from her, and ate. There was more meat. He watched each piece go up to her mouth, watched her tear it for him, and he fed. Taking her food from her fingers. Kate bit the meat into tiny pieces.

She had forgotten she was cold and her skirt was soaked. She had forgotten she was alone and had run away. She had forgotten everything but the need to win the trust of this beautiful animal, and to help him regain his health. The matting mass of blood horrified her. He was very sick.

His fur was dull.

He finished the first slice of meat, crept almost to her side, took the rest of the food from her fingers. Kate determined to make the second slice last even longer, to tear it into even smaller pieces, to gain his confidence.

At last the meal was ended. The cat did not move away. He crouched beside her, and, very gently, Kate touched the soft fur, brushed the tabby head, careful to avoid the gaping mass that, she was sure, would kill him if nothing were done.

The mist was moving. Kate saw the mouth of the cave. The cat looked up at her, his large ears moving backwards and forwards as if he were listening. Tabby stripes on his rounded head; tiger markings on his lean body; white on his muzzle and white on his chest.

Then, slowly and painfully, he eased his body into a stand. He limped back into the mouth of the cave, and Kate followed him. She knew now that this was his shelter and it might shelter her. Would he allow her inside? She crept forwards on hands and knees, feeling every inch of the ground. There was a rocky entrance into a tunnel that twisted and blocked off the wind.

A narrow passage. Unexpectedly, her seeking hand touched the cat and he hissed at her. A warning paw struck at her but he kept his claws sheathed.

Talk to animals, her mother had said. Your voice comforts them; soothes them, steadies them. She had learned to talk to her pony when she went riding, and to their neighbour's bitch. Susie had been a delightful little animal, but she had stayed with her breeder too long and when the Sykes had bought her had been nearly fifteen weeks old. She had lived in a kennel for all that time and was terrified of the world. Kate had helped to reassure her, kneeling by her, stroking her, telling her how good she was and what a wonderful place this was, and that traffic and wind and running water from taps could never hurt her.

Nell Sykes had had no children and been a proxy aunt to Kate. Kate missed her, and her husband, who had been a laughing man, full of jokes, and of stories about his days at sea. He was often away and his wife had been lonely and glad of company. Their house was full of trophies from all over the world. African dolls and masks and spears and warrior shields. A fascinating place for a little girl.

Perhaps she could go back and live with the Sykes. Her father didn't want her. But now the most important thing in the world was to tame the cat so that she could help him and heal that awful wound.

She began to talk, leaning back against the wall, sitting in darkness. She recited the psalms she had had to learn so long ago when she was wrongly accused of cheating. They had beautiful words, comforting words, though they too seemed like stories told to comfort a child.

The world was a brutal place.

"'The Lord is my shepherd, I shall not want.'"

There was no sound from the cat though she was aware of him, crouched beyond her in the darkness, and could hear occasional small movements and a hissed intake of breath.

It would soon be dark outside. She dared not move till the mist cleared and she could see.

More poetry. Kate slipped off her skirt and wrapped herself in the warmth of the fleecy anorak. It came almost to her knees, and when she was crouched, it covered her. It was far too big. It was a good job she had picked that and not one of her own or a thinner coat.

She went on reciting, sitting in the dark, occasionally feeling an odd desire to giggle. Kate McKendrick, marooned in the mist, hiding in a cave, talking to a wild cat. Was he a real wild cat or a farm cat gone wild? It didn't really matter.

The recitations helped her, calmed her, filled in the endless minutes, with all the long night ahead.

"In Hans' old mill the three black cats . . . "

They used to sing that at her other school. Maybe he'd like singing. Kate began to hum very softly.

Time passed so slowly. She felt around her, uncomfortably aware of the rank smell of the place, where the cat had laired now for some weeks. There were bones on the floor. Small bones, which had been picked clean.

She could dimly see the entrance, see into the enveloping mist and the gathering darkness. She would have to stay here till morning.

She curled up inside the anorak, knees drawn up to her chin. The cave was dry and warmer than the outside air. She ate half the chocolate bar, saving the rest for breakfast. She was very hungry now. She lay with her head on her satchel and was so exhausted that she soon slept.

Kate drifted in and out of dreams, unaware that the village had been alerted and that every able man would soon be searching for her. She woke once in the night, to feel against her a warm body. The cat had cuddled up to her, as he too was cold.

"My lion cat," she whispered to him. "I'll take you home and heal you and

144

look after you and you'll be mine for as long as you live. I'll call you Leo."

There was a soft response from the animal. Kate listened in disbelief.

He was purring.

8

SHEINA had driven as fast as she dared over the narrow track, the car twisting and turning, the hairpin bends daring her to be reckless, the loch below her now an angry rumble against the shore. The mist thickened, until driving became a nightmare, peering out into the gloom, creeping over the track until it reached the road; even then it was necessary to travel slowly, as the edge was vague and beyond it the boggy moor that would trap and hold a car.

Kate, Kate, she thought. Why did you have to choose a day like this to run away?

Gavin stared out of the window, his eyes aching. His thoughts tortured him as he saw Kate on the hills, saw Kate falling over the rocky cliffs to lie broken on the rocky shore, or be at the mercy of the driving waves, her drowned face reproaching him for ever.

"Why did she run away?" he asked.

"She came to school; if she had been going away . . . I was angry with her . . . and it wasn't fair."

"Why were you angry? What had she done?"

Sheina slowed even more, and turned into the main road that led to the village police house.

"She recited a poem her mother had loved; in her mother's voice. I couldn't bear it."

"'Windy Nights . . . Whenever the moon and stars are set . . .'" Sheina said.

"She told you?"

"No. It was windy and the children were impossible and I was teaching badly so I read them poetry. And that was the poem I picked."

"You couldn't know," Gavin said. "And she couldn't know."

It was an admission of defeat. An admission that he had failed his child, that he did not know how to help her or himself. The years stretched out before him, lonely and empty of love and companionship.

"It would have been better if her

mother had lived and I had died," Gavin said, the small cabin of the car inviting confidences, the silence of the woman beside him an accepting silence, without accusation. "I'm afraid even to kiss her goodnight in case people think harm."

'Oh God, I hate the world you created,' Sheina said inside her head. She had never thought of that and had a sudden vision of a lonely man, already beset with problems, with that worst problem of all haunting him. Fear of the gossiping tongues that so often lied. She had no idea what to say to him. Comforting words would not help, as she knew as well as he did that small exchanges of affection between a father with an only daughter and no wife might well be interpreted wrongly by the stupid as well as the malicious who sought to hurt.

Hector McBride listened to them both in the comfort of his firelit room, and his wife, small and quiet and very pregnant, brought tea to comfort them, knowing words would not. Outside the window the creeping mist mocked them all.

"It will be difficult tonight, but we can

check around the village. You looked near your home?"

"There wasn't much point," Gavin said. "The mist was too dense. And we have no idea where she might have gone."

Children did not always comfort their parents or please them, Hector thought, as yet knowing nothing of fatherhood. He glanced at his wife, but she was lost in her own world, almost untouched by what went on around her. The babe was due any day now and up to now his only worry had been that she might go into labour tonight and the mist prevent them from getting help.

He did not want to deliver his own child without medical help.

He would have to leave her on her own and organise a search. Perhaps their neighbour would come and sit with her. He and Gavin walked outside. The mist was thicker than ever.

"We can do nothing in this," Hector said. "We don't even know where to start. I'll ring for help and we'll get the dogs out by morning. They at least might follow her trail even though the mist hides the hills."

"Ye can't go home," Morag said. "Neither of you. Not in this. With darkness and the mist ye might go right off the road. Miss McDonald can sleep in our spare room and maybe Mr McKendrick would not mind the settee? It will be warm down here."

Gavin didn't care where he slept. He would not sleep. He would lie, his thoughts needling him, his conscience destroying him, thinking of Kate out there on the wild moors, or worse, far away, at the mercy of a madman. If anything happened to her. He could not bear that thought either.

He was grateful to Hector who, when the women had gone to bed, pulled up his own chair and produced glasses and malt whisky, which he poured in generous measure, and lit his pipe.

"As a medicine," he said. "And what would you be doing here, Mr McKendrick? Is it a long holiday you are having?"

"I'm filming the Golden Eagles," Gavin said. "I've been trying to keep that quiet. I don't know if the local people know about the nest. I was afraid of people coming to watch and making the birds leave their young."

"What will you do with the film?"

"It was commissioned by one of the television companies. I've some grand shots. Of one of the eggs hatching. And the young eagle crying for food. And the parents bringing back green twigs to stick in that untidy bundle of a nest."

"Two eggs hatched. Are they rearing both?"

"One fell out of the nest and died on the rocks below, before it was even four days old," Gavin said.

Hector nodded.

"Aye, it's nearly always like that. The stronger hatchling pushes the younger out of the nest, as there is not always enough food. Nature is cruel. I used to watch that eyrie when I was a boy, climbing the high hill above them to look down through the glasses my grandfather lent me. It was the same every year. Only one reared, though two might hatch. I found the tiny bodies, time and again. I never knew them rear two."

He drew on his pipe thoughtfully. Blue

smoke wreathed his hand and reminded Gavin brutally of the mist outside, and Kate alone and cold, and maybe lying dead at the foot of the rocks. If only he hadn't shouted at her. If only he could go back and live yesterday again.

The peat was a black cave with a deep red glow in its heart. The room was warm, and Gavin was exhausted. He was also, he realised, extremely hungry in spite of his worries. He had not eaten since lunchtime and that was over twelve hours ago. The crawling hands of the clock showed ten past one.

"When did you discover Kate had gone?" asked Hector. He had often noticed the child in her odd clothes when he passed the school. She was always alone, standing looking through the railings as if she felt imprisoned. Sheina's story had been incomplete and she had not explained how she had driven to Kate's cottage and met Gavin on his way home.

"Miss McDonald came to look for me. She was waiting at the cottage. We went in and looked for Kate there, but she hadn't been home at all. So we came straight here, but the mist delayed us. It took nearly two hours to drive here."

They had arrived just before seven o'clock. They ate early so that Hector's wife could go early to her bed. The policeman looked at Gavin. The man would not have fed, nor the woman either, but maybe Morag had made her food and not thought about him.

He stood up stiffly, a big man, with reddish hair that curled close to his head and bright blue eyes that often laughed but that now regarded his unexpected guest with concern.

He went out of the room, and Gavin watched the peat fire flicker and turn to ash. He did not look up as Hector returned, and was startled when the man laid a tray on the table beside him. Thick-cut bread, well buttered, filled with pickle and cold meat and some with cheese.

A pot of hot coffee. Buttered scones with strawberry jam, and a slice of currant cake.

"Ye'll feel better with food inside ye." Hector poured the coffee into hand-thrown brown mugs patterned with black geese. He piled sandwiches on to a small matching plate and passed it across to Gavin.

"I can eat any time of the day or night," Hector said, and helped himself.

Gavin had needed the food. He stretched wearily when his host had gone to bed, and pulled the warm tartan rug over him. The room was hot, but would be cold by dawn when the fire had gone, Hector said.

There were pictures in the dying flames. Memories that were best forgotten but that flared as the fire flared, and then vanished to be replaced by others. Memories of Kate as a tiny girl. She had thought him a hero then, invincible, able to command the storm and stop the thunder and shut off the lightning and bid the rain to cease so that she could go out to play.

She had curled up on his lap like a little cat, warm and trusting. They had made such plans for her, he and Margaret.

The clock ticked on, a dragging unhurried sound, reminding him of time passing too slowly.

At last he slept.

He woke to find Hector at his side with a cup of tea, and an offer of the bathroom and a shower and a shave.

"We have all the amenities here, with the electricity," the policeman said. "Not like your little home on the moors."

"We do have electricity, but from a generator, and we certainly don't have all mod cons. The bathroom is a bit primitive though there's running water. It's an ancient bath."

Hector walked to the window and lifted the curtain. "The mist is breaking and the dogs are on their way."

"Can they follow her?"

"Donald who is in charge of them says there is a possibility. Her trail will be old, more than eighteen hours old, but moisture holds the scent. One of the dogs is very experienced, a dog named Troy. There's always a chance. We never give up hope."

Not until we have to, he said inside his head, as Gavin went out of the room to shower and shave.

Hector glanced at his wife as she came

in carrying a tray loaded for the table. He took it from her.

"You ought not to be carrying that."

She laughed at him.

"The baby's not due for another week yet, and it will probably be late. My mother was late with all three of us, and my sister was late with young Rory too. Don't fret." She spread the flowered cloth and laid the mats and knives and forks.

Sheina, coming down the stairs, went into the kitchen to help and Hector listened to the soft voices, and the occasional laugh. Morag could make a deaf man laugh if she chose.

"We've made piles of sandwiches," Sheina said. "I'll have to go to school, but can Mr McKendrick come out and help you? He needs to be occupied. Dear knows how long the search will take."

Or how it will end, she thought, and, remembering the laughter in the kitchen, felt guilty. Oh Kate, Kate, you little fool. Why did you have to run away? She would never be able to keep her mind on teaching today.

Gavin was impatient to start but was

156

made to sit and eat a plate of eggs and bacon, with sausage and fried potatoes to follow. Hunger went on, come hell or despair. But what did Kate have to eat?

The police dog vans were outside. Voices rose in the hall, and Hector brought in three large men who overfilled the small room, and who grinned at Morag. "Not had that baby yet?" asked one of them. "It's been coming for ever."

"Seems longer than that," Morag said, offering plates of hot rolls filled with bacon to the men while Hector poured out mugs of coffee.

They ate and looked at the map on the wall, and the ways that led from the school. Would she have made for home? Or had she accepted a lift from a stranger? Or was she somewhere between home and school, sheltering? Or would they find a broken child, who had left the world behind her for ever? That was a thought in everyone's mind, but no one spoke it. You hoped until the last possible moment proved you terribly wrong.

The last remnants of rolls were crammed into ever hungry mouths.

These men were so young, Gavin thought in sudden despair. To them this was just another job. How could they know how he felt? He followed them out to the vans, and, as he lowered himself into the passenger seat of the leading vehicle, he was greeted by a crescendo of barking from behind him as the two police dogs gave tongue, guarding their territory from the intruder.

"Settle down, Venn, Troy," the handler said. "You're going to need all your energy. There's a job to do."

The two German Shepherds quieted once the engine roared to life. Gavin turned to look at them. Dark heads watched him, ears pricked, brown eyes brilliant in the dark of the small compartment. They were handsome animals. Long lines and harnesses hung on the mesh that kept the dogs secure.

The last wraiths of mist blew away on the wind. The sky was grey, lowering almost to the treetops. Gavin stared out of the window.

He knew they would never find Kate in all that wildness. Where would they look? Miles of desolate moors, ravines and gullies, and below the cliffs the surging sea that might have carried her away to fling her unrecognised on a distant beach. Children did vanish, sometimes for ever.

"We'll find her, sir," his driver said, with more confidence than he felt, and accelerated towards the school that was to be their starting point.

9

THE wind blew the last shreds of mist away. Kate, exhausted, slept on. The cat, weak with pain, lay quietly against her, savouring her warmth. The rising sun threw half shadows across the little cave.

The search party had started as soon as it was light. Gavin watched as the dogs were taken out, and harnessed.

"Don't they need something of Kate's to get her scent?" he asked.

The dog handler laughed.

"They have to learn to pick up a scent without that. Murderers and burglars don't usually leave calling cards. We take the dogs along the roads Kate might have used and if she struck off somewhere on her own, they'll soon pick up a trail. They won't find one if there are dozens of conflicting trails, though, or if she used a well beaten track that others have used since."

Gavin looked out at the moors and

the hills. Far overhead an eagle circled lazily but he barely noticed it. His mind was concentrated on Kate, and he was praying unconsciously all the time.

Please God, let her be safe.

Perhaps someone had taken her in for the night and would persuade her to come home. Where would she have gone?

The dogs were fanned out around the school grounds, heads down. They appeared to be doing nothing. One of the men went to the end of the road, and along it to a little lane that led to the moors behind.

"That could lead her to a short cut home," Hector said.

"We'll find her, sir, never fear," a voice said in his ear, and Gavin turned to see a man in postman's uniform beside him. Grey hair and a round face and kind eyes that looked straight at him. "I know the little lass. We often have a wee chat when I bring the mail. She'll be all right. Just lost in the mist and sensibly sheltering. She's a wise wee girl."

There were other men there too. Gavin knew none of them, but felt a warmth towards them, taking the trouble to help him search. Several women, dressed in thick coats and wellingtons, had joined them, and the policeman in charge of the party was giving directions.

Soon the hillside was alive with small figures, searching every crack in the ground, every hollow, under every bush. Searching, Gavin was suddenly sure, with a sickening feeling inside him, not for a live girl, but for a dead body.

"Hey, 'ey," one of the dog handlers said. "Troy's found something."

The dog was pulling strongly on his line, his handler almost running. Gavin watched as the animal climbed the hill, zigzagging in an oddly erratic path.

Up through new growing heather and bracken; across a sheep trail, and up the shoulder of the hill to a spot immediately under the eagle's eyrie. The birds were agitated now, and both were soaring, and watching, anxious for their nest and their one fledgling.

Gavin watched them. It would have made good filming, but the film no longer mattered. Nothing mattered except Kate. He had not realised how much he left her alone; how isolated she must feel.

They had been climbing gently for two hours. The mood of the little group had become increasingly grim, although both Hector and a second dog handler were sure that Troy was on a trail that would lead them successfully to their goal.

She couldn't have run this far, Gavin thought.

The dog hesitated and circled. Then struck off again in almost the opposite direction to that he had been following, and began, more confidently, to edge round the hill, following an apparently crazy path among the tumbled rocks. The ground between them was turf, bright with flowers.

The dog reached the cave, and barked.

Kate woke to see a huge head framed in the cave opening. The cat, electrified, found strength to spring to his feet, to stand, snarling, fur fluffed up, tail bushed, and then, with a hiss of hate, he fled to the back of the cave and vanished down a narrow crack too small for Kate to follow.

She crouched, terrified.

"Are you there, Kate?" a voice called,

and a man's head appeared beside the dog. "Good boy, Troy. Very clever boy."

A wet tongue was licking her face. "Come on, love. He won't hurt you. Your dad's been looking for you and he's very worried about you. Are you all right? Nobody's hurt you?"

Kate shook her head. She was stiff and cold, and very hungry. She crept out into the light, and stood blinking. Once she was used to the brightness, she was startled to see how many people were standing, watching her.

"Kate!" Her father ran towards her, and hugged her. "Why did you run away? Are you all right?"

Kate could think of nothing but the cat. He needed food. He needed help and he had run away from them all. He would never trust her again. He would die in the cave, out of reach of people, as no human could go through the narrow crack that he had found.

She could say nothing. She felt as if she had been turned to stone. She was numbed from all the emotion of the past hours, and bewildered at the thought of all those people looking for her and all the trouble she had caused.

One of the policemen brought a blanket and wrapped it round her. She looked up at him, her face dirty and streaked with tears. She tried to walk, but her legs seemed to belong to someone else. The world seemed very far away and to grow small and remote, and misty.

Her father caught her as she fell.

"Take her home," one of the women said. "Get her to bed and keep her warm. I'll send the doctor over. It's too far to the hospital."

Gavin carried his daughter down the hillside. One of the police cars was waiting. He sat in the back, cradling her, looking at the small tear-stained face, cursing himself for his neglect of her. He would never forgive himself. Would she ever forgive him?

★ ★ ★

It was lunchtime before Sheina heard the news that Kate was safe. She had a free afternoon and had intended to go out and join the search party. Hector called in to tell her all was well, or as well as it might be. There was a lot wrong with the child mentally and emotionally. Kate had recovered enough to walk up to her bed, but she lay there, refusing to speak to anyone, tears pouring down her face.

"Hasn't she said anything?" Sheina asked. Hector too was distracted. Morag had started with labour pains and was on her way to the hospital. And he wasn't free to join her.

"Just one thing when she came out of the faint, or whatever it was. She said, 'The cat will die. We must save the cat.'"

"A cat? Was she delirious?"

Hector shrugged.

"Should I go over? Would I be welcome? Or in the way?" Sheina asked. She could not settle to anything that afternoon. She needed to know what had happened, needed to see Kate, needed to find out if she could help.

"They need a woman there. The place is a tip," Hector said. "The man rarely there, the child doing her best and she only a baby herself, and no mother to help her or care for her or smooth her way."

He thought of his own baby, so soon to be born. And Morag, whom he could not live without. Some men were too unlucky.

Sheina drove over, her mind busy with possibilities. Had Kate hit her head and been raving? Had she imagined or dreamed a cat? How could there be a cat up there on the hill? Hector had said they found her in a little cave, not far below the eagle's nest. She must have walked for miles.

The cottage was small and lopsided, its roof appearing to slip towards the ground. Sheina had never known Gavin's father. The old vet must have died at least six years ago, if not more, and he had been ill for some time before that. His wife had died two years before he did. Sheina remembered that the history master had mentioned him one afternoon. Some of the sixth formers were doing a project on the growth of the village, from the end of the Second World War, focusing on its more memorable residents. They remembered taking their animals to Kate's grandfather when they were small, and spoke about him still.

He had been quite a character, ready to come out on the wildest night, always available and always concerned, even about a rabbit or a gerbil or a hamster.

Maybe they didn't realise Kate was his granddaughter. They might have made her more welcome.

Far below the water sparkled blue, and far above a lone bird circled, and flew towards the top of the hill. White tops on the waves and white gulls crying, making the scene even more desolate. What a place to bring a child, Sheina thought. There all alone when she isn't at school and no one at all to talk to.

A fire blazed in the grate. The inside was brighter and better than she had expected, but the furniture, though adequate for a seaside holiday, seemed to reveal that this was indeed a temporary home.

There had been an auction of the furniture when the old man died. Bridie's furniture had gone to her niece. There was little to remind her of a home. No ornaments. No pictures on the walls. Kate had done her best to keep it clean, and there were wild flowers in a jam jar on the window sill. The place lacked a soul.

How could the man live here with a child? The room was untidy with books, with clothes, and with papers. The curtains needed a wash. There was spilled food on the cooker and unwashed dishes sat in the sink. Sheina itched to start cleaning.

"I came to see if I could help," she said.

"I don't know what to do. She won't speak. The only thing she has said is about a cat. We never had a cat."

The man sounded bewildered. He was totally adrift, unable to judge how to comfort his child. A waif himself, Sheina thought and was furious with herself. He needed kicking, not pity. He had that for himself. Had he ever thought of his daughter or her feelings?

She went upstairs. Kate had sobbed herself to exhaustion and lay, staring at the ceiling. It was a tiny room with a sloping roof and a small window that no one had cleaned in years. At least the bed looked comfortable, and the bedclothes were clean, and the blankets warm.

The child's clothes hung on a rail that was the only wardrobe. Not a decent thing among them. Gavin had had little interest in furnishing the place to let and the budget had been limited.

"Kate? What cat?"

Kate stared at her.

"He lives on the hill. He's beautiful. My wild tiger. Someone's shot him; his shoulder; it's septic. The dog frightened him. He was lying in my arms. I wanted to bring him home, to make him better. Only he's gone, into a tiny crack and I can't reach him; no one will reach him. He'll die there, and I can't help him."

"A wild cat?" She had heard that there had been one stalking the hill. It would be Donald McLeod who had shot at it. Donald hated cats and wild cats most of all. He was anxious for his grouse. There were also blackcock, which were still rare and were being re-introduced. The cat was a threat to the chicks. But maybe it would confine itself to rabbits

170

and hares and perhaps the fish left in the tide pools.

Kate nodded.

"He was coming for food. I wanted to tame him. To bring him to live with me."

It was Friday evening and the weekend ahead. She had made no plans. Her own affairs could wait. The shadow of night was hiding the sunset. It was no use hunting now, but maybe in the morning.

"Tomorrow," Sheina said. "You can show me where he is and we'll take food. I can ask the vet for a cage for him, a trap cage that won't hurt him, with a door that will drop and keep him safe. Food inside it, and then we can take him to the vet for him to look at that injury. We can put him in the shed, make a safe place for him, or make a cage for him. He's wild, Kate. I doubt he'd ever settle, but we can maybe heal him and let him free again. He might come to you for food at times; he would never ever stay."

"I just want him well again." The tears were rolling down the child's cheeks, but she cried silently, hopelessly. Sheina sat on the edge of her bed and gathered the small body against her, hugging her tightly, feeling a mixture of emotions wash over her. Deprived motherhood maybe, and anger at the man who was so careless of this small life that he could leave her alone, day after day, to follow his own whims.

Surely he could have taken her with him?

The sobs ceased. Sheina, looking down, saw that Kate was asleep. She covered her. The pillowslip needed changing. She hunted in a cupboard in the bathroom and found a clean one, ready to replace it when Kate woke. Surely the child didn't do all the housekeeping here?

Gavin was standing by the fire, looking at his daughter's diary. He had not intended to do so, but it had been lying open on the battered couch, and he had picked it up idly, thinking it a school book.

"She's been watching the eagles," he said. "I didn't think she knew about them. She's made notes. 'The soaring

172

birds cry, eldritch shrieks that frighten the air and echo from the crags. They drop and from the heather comes a dying scream, as some small creature perishes to keep their hungry young.

" 'There's a dead nestling on the hill. The first hatched may have pushed him out. Nature is very cruel.' I didn't know she'd found it. I looked, but never came across it. It was pushed from the nest between its fourth and fifth day."

He sighed.

"They rarely rear two. Kate's right. Life is cruel."

"Kate said nature, not life." Sheina looked about her, wondering if there were food in the cottage. "You could have taken her with you. Not left her alone. Who did she talk to? Who did she play with? Who ever visited? What did she do with herself, while you were up there on the crags?"

"I was filming," Gavin said defensively. "We need to eat."

"She could have helped you; been part of it. Not left to her own devices. Her only friend a wild cat that's injured. We're going to try and find it in the morning. Try to heal it. Nothing else will help her."

"Her mother would have known what to do. I don't. I don't know anything about children . . . they baffle me. Kate baffles me. She doesn't talk to me; I don't know what she wants or what she thinks." There was desperation in his voice.

"Did you talk to her? She wants what other children want. Laughter and companionship. Something or someone to love. She could do with some pretty clothes. Nothing she has fits her and the other children mock her and laugh at her because of it. What sort of life do you think she's led here?"

She wished she had said nothing. She had not realised that the bottled thoughts of the last two months had been so bitter. She had never imagined that any face could show such dismay. The anger died, leaving a helpless pity that was alien to her.

Gavin stared at her, and she felt as if she had hit him.

"Let me tidy the place up. You're exhausted. And I'll make a meal for us

174

both. Have you eaten at all today?"

He shook his head.

Sheina started with the little kitchen, exploring, finding chops and potatoes and frozen peas in the minute deep freeze on top of the refrigerator. There was a washing machine. Outside the generator buzzed continuously and irritatingly and the yellow lights flickered, sometimes dimming almost to dark and then flaring briefly.

"You can't have everything working at once," Gavin said.

The stove was powered by calor gas. She lit the burners, and began to cook. She cleaned the sink, and scrubbed the draining board and table. She loved home making and longed to fill the place with more colour, with pictures on the walls, with ornaments on the sideboard and the mantelpiece. With shelves for the books.

"I'd like to take Kate to find the cat; to go to the vet with him and have him treated. And then to buy her some decent clothes. May I?" Sheina asked, after dishing the food on to plates, as they started to eat. "It will mean a trip to the town. Have you any plans for her?"

"No plans," Gavin said.

"Would you like to come?"

He shook his head. He had watched uneasily as she tidied and cleaned, suddenly seeing the place through her eyes. The makeshift home, a holiday place, not a permanent base. Somewhere to pause briefly and then move on. The untidiness. He had meant to buy bookshelves, to find furniture to store the clutter, but the days had passed, and there had never been enough time.

"What are you going to do when you've finished the film?"

"I hadn't thought that far. I've sold our old home. I put all the furniture in store. There's too much for this place. I only came here to film the eagles. I don't know where I want to live. Not here. It's too remote. I don't know how I'm going to work. There's no one to look after Kate if I get foreign assignments, and those are the ones that pay."

Sheina hesitated. She didn't want involvement, but the thought of the child here alone, of the man who had no desire to put down roots, overcame her reluctance.

"The cottage makes a base. One you could come back to, even if you don't always live here. It needs more furniture, and some bits and pieces for Kate; little ornaments to make it a home, not just somewhere to stay. While you are here, you could bring her to me in the morning; she could come to me in the evening while you're working. That would make far more sense."

She hesitated again, wondering if the man thought her interfering.

"Are you keeping this as a base? Or selling it when the film's complete?" Maybe she shouldn't press him, but she needed to know, for her own peace of mind. She couldn't bear to think of Kate adrift for the next few years, while she was growing up.

"I don't know. I grew up here. I was happy here, once. I meant to look up old friends, but I haven't had the heart to visit anyone . . . I haven't been able to make up my mind about anything. It doesn't seem to matter where we live."

"I don't think you ought to uproot

Kate again. A child who drifts from school to school, staying nowhere for long, never puts down roots or makes friends. She has no chance. Keep the cottage, and when you're away, Kate can come to me. I've plenty of room and she'd be no bother. Be company for me," she added, hoping that might make Gavin agree.

It was a solution and he grabbed at anything that could help him make amends for the past months. Sheina felt as if she had found two stray animals on the hill, just as Kate had found the wild cat. She was getting involved when she had vowed not to be.

But what was life about if you always stayed on the sidelines and allowed no one close?

She spent the evening cleaning and tidying. Books stacked neatly and clothes folded and put away, with those that needed washing ready for next day.

She looked in at Kate before she left. The child was sleeping, her face shadowed, as if she dreamed bad dreams.

Outside the cottage the moon slid through the clouds, a thin moon, a new moon, and on an impulse she wished. She did not know if her wish were to alien gods or a prayer to a God who might be somewhere in the unimaginable mystery that had provoked this universe.

"Let the cat live; let me help these two. Let there be a better life for Kate, a future she will enjoy. Help me to help them wisely."

A cloud drifted across the moonslip. Was it an answer or a denial? Gavin thanked her, awkwardly, unused to speaking socially to women other than his wife. She recognised the shyness for what it was and smiled up at him.

"Will you at least think about my idea? It would be much pleasanter for Kate. You can collect her at bedtime if you are filming during the evening, on these light nights. And I could ask other children to meet her. It would help them accept her."

"It's a lot to ask. I'd be imposing."

"I thought by now I'd be married," Sheina said. "He thought differently. My life is lonely too. You'd be doing me a favour."

And so, she thought, he would. Kate would liven her life. She liked the child, could love the child, could maybe love the man . . .

She was being ridiculous.

"Thank you. Can we talk tomorrow? I'd like to think. The baby eagle flies twelve weeks after hatching; I must make plans for the future. Maybe I could film the island life; find other themes here. Stay here for a while myself, and stop travelling."

He was exhausted, Sheina thought, and needed to rest awhile, to heal himself, and in healing, he would also heal Kate.

"Kate would like that, I think. Tomorrow," she said.

She was aware of him as she eased herself into her car and switched on the lights that flooded the road in front of her.

"I've kept you." His voice apologised although his words did not.

"No problem. I'm used to that. Until tomorrow. I'll be over early. Make sure Kate has had something decent to eat."

She couldn't help bossing, she thought wryly, as she let in the clutch.

He stood framed in the light of the cottage door, watching the car drive away. She knew he was watching her, and wondered what he made of her intrusion and her interference.

'Never interfere. It's not wanted or liked.' Her mother's voice came back to her. Her mother never had interfered. Which was wise? Never to hold out an offer of help or a hand to someone in distress, or to try, and find that the help was in vain, was unwanted all the time, and only accepted because the recipient did not know how to refuse?

"I have to try," she told the moon as she locked her car. Beyond her cottage the faint light glinted on the hills. Out there was Kate's cat. They'd look for him and find him. It was the first time for months that she felt as if her life had any real purpose.

Suddenly elated, she went indoors.

10

THE cat lay still for a long time after the noises had ceased. He had been drowned in scent. Terrifying scent from men and from the dog. Loud voices, and noises from unseen creatures, as well as that overwhelming tang that brought fear, drove him through the narrow gap to crouch, his heart racing, his ears moving backwards and forwards, till silence settled again on the hill.

Pain was now part of his life. He had forgotten how it felt to be free of the throb in his shoulder. He tried to lick at it, but the injury was beyond help and his tongue did little but remind him of the hurt.

He was in a tiny cave at the back of the crack. Room, just, to crouch, to turn round, but not to stand or to stretch himself. The rock pressed against his back. The faint light vanished, and all was dark until a finger of moonlight shone across his head.

He was on the road to death, but it was a long road and a slow road and his body still clamoured for life. For food. Hunger dominated him, and so did thirst. Even so, death was very near, and within a couple of days, the cat would give up the struggle. He would be too weak to find food.

He needed to move, to hunt, but as he tried to creep through the crack, there came a sound from the darkness outside. He did not know what was prowling till he caught the sharp musky fox tang and heard the sniffing nose. The fox, in passing, had caught the scent of blood. But he was full fed, having just finished with a young hare that lay unwary in the bracken and could not run fast enough to escape the biting jaws.

He paused, paw upraised, to consider, and then loped on. The cat, knowing he had no strength in him to fight, crouched low, and dozed, and woke and dozed again, and his life force ebbed even further from him, but he was not yet ready to give up.

* * *

Kate came downstairs early, impatient to be away, and to find the cat. She looked a waif child, large eyed, blue circles showing her exhaustion. She was wary of her father still, afraid he would scold her for running away. She had caused a lot of trouble and guilt had added to her fears for the cat. If only they could go home, go back in time, have her mother alive. Her mother would have understood. But if her mother had been alive none of this would have happened.

Gavin watched his daughter, his own expression that of helpless bewilderment. He had stopped thinking about himself and his own frustration and misery.

He could only think of Kate and the days she had been left alone. He saw the cottage through Sheina's eyes, good enough for an odd fortnight spent fishing or shooting, but very far from being a home.

He could have taken the child into his confidence, could have taken her to the hide, but he had wanted to nurse his misery, unable to bear her chatter. He had been thinking of her as a child still; and she had grown up so much.

He wanted to talk to her, wanted to hug her, wanted to show his regret, tell her that he cared desperately for her, but he did not know what to say.

He could only sit helplessly and watch her and pay for his past neglect by suffering the needling guilt that had overtaken him since he first heard that Kate was missing from school.

Kate could not eat. She picked at her breakfast and Gavin watched her, trying to see into her mind. She could not tell him she was afraid the cat would die. She could not bear the cat to die. He had crept into the space left in her heart after her mother had died.

He had become part of her life. She saw him, in full health, his great eyes watching her. Saw him crouched, in the hidden recess of the cave; felt his body against hers, heard the sudden rasping purr with which he had greeted her when she woke to find him pressed against her.

It had been a long lonely time, when she was lost and he had been her only reassurance. Then, when she had been found, everyone seemed to want to fuss her and it bewildered her. The police, even the postman, the village women who had helped in the search, the men expressing their relief that she was safe.

She was unused to so much attention from anyone. Her days had been spent alone; her time at school had been a misery to be endured, and Sheina had merely been her teacher. Kinder than most, but with only a small significance in her life. More than most people, admittedly, but Kate had become self-sufficient, a solitary child, feeling forgotten by all the world.

Except the wild cat. That had wanted her, had briefly needed her, and she longed for its companionship for the rest of its life.

Sheina had also spent the night worrying. She had not intended to become involved. She was not even sure she liked the man, but the overwhelming pity she felt for the child was the pity that had induced her to rescue a stray dog, long ago, to work for neglected animals, to spend time on children that others gave up as hopeless cases.

She had not done that since she came

to this school. She had vowed never to be involved again. Never to be hurt again. Life was easier if you were an onlooker, always watching, never a participant.

Now she had involved herself, and with a couple of misfits. The man seemed to be an emotional cripple, and his attitude had affected the child. She was as wary as the wild cat, as likely to run off. Sheina, half awake and half asleep, tossing restlessly as the moon slipped down the sky, found she had identified the child and the animal almost as one entity.

Perhaps the child had adopted the cat because they were so alike. Two solitary individuals, living their lives in such a way that humans only touched them briefly. Kate, wandering the hills alone at weekends and after school on the light nights; the cat always alone, a symbol of strength, enjoying his wildness.

She had fallen asleep long after midnight, to dream that she had a huge cage and was trying to entice Kate into it. The child watched her, wary, crouched, and when Sheina walked forward she hissed and spat and turned into a wild cat, and sprang.

Sheina woke sweating, thankful that the sun had lightened the sky and the day could begin. She planned it as she drove to the cottage, over the long narrow road that twisted through the desolate moors. The eagle was briefly overhead, and then she was descending towards the loch and Kate was waiting for her at the gate, impatient to find the wild cat.

"We start at the vet's," Sheina said. "Ruaraidh McVeigh is a friend of mine. He has borrowed a special cage from another friend who traps wild animals for zoos. We take the cat to him. OK?"

Kate nodded.

"Go out to my car. I want a word with your Dad."

Gavin looked as if he had braced himself for a confrontation but Sheina only asked a question.

"When's Kate's birthday?"

He stared at her.

"Last month. I forgot."

"Then you remember. Can I take her and buy her some decent clothes, and perhaps something she wants to put on the mantelpiece in her bedroom;

188

something to make it hers? There's nothing here. Did you put everything in store?"

"Yes. I planned, later, to send it all to the auction rooms. I wanted to forget," Gavin said.

"Did Kate have no choice?"

"She has her books. She's a bit old for her old toys."

"I still have my teddy bear," Sheina said. "And ornaments that people have given me as presents. My memories."

She saw his expression and wished she hadn't spoken.

She watched him walk to the table, too old for his years. An exhausted man, unable to cope with his present situation. Only eighteen months away from the death of his wife, grief not yet forgotten, nor worked out. He wrote out a cheque, leaving the total blank, and handed it to her.

"You can go up to four hundred pounds," he said. "She needs everything new. Is that enough? Can you shop in one place?"

"I can cash it and then we can shop where Kate chooses," Sheina said. "I'll keep her with me till the evening meal. Come to my house and we'll eat there. Then you can take her home afterwards."

He had been working in a fog, only half aware of the world around him. He felt like a man waking from a drugged sleep and the waking was painful.

He nodded his thanks, wishing he could find words to tell her how much her help meant, but he had never been a man who found speech easy. He might, in his happier days, tease, or mock, and hope that his hearer knew that this hid thoughts that he would have felt it unmanly to speak. Funny face, to him, was an endearment.

He watched as Sheina slid in behind the wheel, watched as she spoke to his daughter, watched the small face light up with sudden ecstasy. A day out, and new clothes, and the cat would be safe and the vet would heal him.

The journey to the vet's house seemed endless, but at last they arrived. The cage was ready.

"Soak it in your scent," Ruaraidh said. "Fill it with your old clothes. Put your clothes over it and around it. Rub it,

190

inside and out, with your hands. He trusts you. He won't trust other people. He ran from them in terror. And put this skinned rabbit inside it, and leave it close to the cave. If you can, close to the crack at the back. I know that crack; it leads nowhere, into a tiny place that he can only just turn in. I used to play there as a child. My torch shone through that crack on so many occasions, trying to see if it went anywhere. It doesn't. The cage is bigger than the crack and he will have to come out sometime."

Or die there, he thought, wondering about that festered shoulder, and whether gangrene had developed.

"We may not be able to help him, Kate." The words were a warning, but Kate was beginning to believe in miracles. He knew she did not believe him, and watched from the window as the child ran out to the car, holding the cage as if it were a talisman.

It was an odd day. A new beginning for both of them. Kate had made awkward conversation at breakfast, and Gavin had tried to recapture some of the closeness that had once been between them. He thought about it as he climbed the hill, anxious to capture the soaring birds on film.

Kate sat, the skinned rabbit joints on her lap in a dish which she held tightly. She had the clothes that she had worn yesterday, to reassure him, as he now knew her scent.

There was no sign of movement on the hill. The sun, untimely hot, burned down on the heather that yesterday had been soaked with rain. The sea shone blue, reflecting a cloudless sky.

Kate could not sort her thoughts. She was excited at the prospect of new clothes and a day in the town, but the niggling worry was there, all the time. Was the cat alive? Would he come to the cage? Or was he so weak he couldn't come back through the crack? Would the vet be able to heal him? She remembered the wound and shivered. It would have got worse. Septic injuries never healed by themselves. Suppose he had blood poisoning?

She couldn't tell Sheina. It would sound silly.

Kate removed the clothing and laid it

in the cave. She placed the cage against the crack, the rabbit joints on the wooden floor. The front was so balanced that it would drop as the cat went inside. They wedged the cage with two big boulders so that it was immovable.

"He might not be in there," Sheina said. "He might have left it during the night. Don't hope too much, Kate."

Even if he were there, Kate had a new worry. "How will the vet be able to touch him if he's so terrified?"

"With a tranquillising dart. That part's easy, Kate. It's what comes after. He's wild, remember, and has no reason to trust anyone. We'll have to make him a cage to live in while he heals. And when he's better, he'll have to go free, back to the life he knows. He'll never settle in a human home."

Kate's dream of a cat lying on her bed, a cat to cuddle and love, drifted away on a sigh. She knew that Sheina was right. But perhaps the cat would settle. Perhaps everyone was wrong. He had come to her; he would stay with her. God wouldn't let him die.

But God had let her mother die.

Sheina wished she knew what the child was thinking. Kate's expression was sombre again.

"We'll leave now. And come back later to get him, if he's there. Put your clothes behind the cage, close against it. He may remember your smell. He slept close to you once; he may come again, hoping for warmth. He will have food, once he is trapped, and though the cage will alarm him, he may settle to sleep. It must be days since he fed properly if his shoulder is as bad as you say."

Kate looked back at the dark entrance of the cave and wondered if the cat were inside. Maybe if the dog hadn't come, he would have followed her down the hillside and home. She wasn't really lost. As soon as daylight came, she knew where she was. Would she have gone home? She didn't know. Her father didn't really want her. Only his filming and his eagles.

The cat was all she had.

11

KATE had seen the little town only briefly, when she and her father arrived. They had driven through in the late evening. The village shops stocked all their needs, and Gavin hated busy places. The school was between the village and the town, on its outskirts. Kate, travelling to and fro on the school bus, had never had time to explore beyond the playground walls.

Sheina determined to salvage the day and turn it into an adventure. She talked of the clothes they might buy, as she drove over the moors, along the winding road that bordered the loch. There was orange wrack along the beaches and the sharp tang of seaweed.

"My grandfather used to sing a song about the tangle of the Isles," Kate said, as Sheina negotiated the last steep hill before the sprawling town. "He said it healed."

"It does." Sheina thought of quiet days

on the beach, watching seals bask in the sun and the seabirds whirl and cry. Remembered drowning her own bitter memories in peace and the sounds of small waves breaking against the rocks.

Then they were in the town and Kate, who had forgotten large shops, could not believe that she could spend so much money, all on herself. For a few brief hours her mood lightened, and Sheina saw the child Kate once had been, eyes alight with excitement, as all the pretty clothes were spread for her to see.

The assistant was as eager as Sheina to make Kate's choice happy. They selected blue jeans and tartan trews; bright jerseys, patterned and plain. A blue dress, with a whirling skirt, and tights and smart black slippers. A warm anorak, padded, with a hood to keep off the rain. Gloves and two tartan woollen caps. Dark skirts and white blouses and jackets for school, where there was no uniform.

"Can I wear something now? Something that fits?" Kate asked wistfully. The too tight jeans and her father's cast off jersey lay on the fitting room chair. She didn't want to put them on again.

Sheina, caught up in the child's excitement, laughed.

They chose blue jeans and a jersey patterned with Siamese cats. Blue and white trainers, that Kate had longed to wear and her father had never bought for her, and the dark blue anorak that was striped with scarlet to match the jersey.

At lunchtime, after having her hair cut into a neat sleek cap, they ate fish and chips, which Kate had decided was the most exciting meal she could think of. It was something they never had at home now. It reminded her of her mother, and holiday lunches when Kate slipped down the road to the chippie, and brought the food back, hot and delicious smelling, and they ate out of the newspaper, to save washing up.

Those picnic meals had been fun. Her father never knew about them. In those far away days he would have disapproved, and insisted on hot plates and sitting at the table, instead of sitting on the floor on the hearthrug, laughing and talking. Yet at the cottage he had never bothered about laying the table, and often they sat by the fire, and ate, balancing the plates on their knees.

Throughout the day, Kate's thoughts reverted to the cat, sick and alone, creeping out of his hiding place to savour the food she had brought, and then lying there, trapped and terrified, unable to escape.

"Have you a name for the cat?" Sheina asked.

"I called him Leo, but it isn't right for him. He needs another name; a grand name. He's so beautiful."

Sheina was determined that the day should be memorable. There was one last call to make, at her favourite shop, before leaving for the hill. Kate looked in disbelief at the shelves full of model animals; cats and dogs, horses and seals, badgers and foxes. Small birds balanced on china branches; four sheepdogs lay together on a grassy knoll on a shining wooden plaque.

"Your father says you can come to me in the morning and stay with me in the evening until he comes for you." Sheina was watching the child's face, hoping for a hint of excitement. Kate looked back at her, expressionless, giving no hint as to her own thoughts. Sheina sighed. Children were inexplicable. "Why don't you buy something for your bedroom? A picture, or an ornament. A belated birthday present, your father said."

That did spark a reaction. Kate looked up at her with delight in her eyes and the woman thought the lie worth while. She watched the child dance through the shop on quicksilver feet, transformed by a little thought and attention, temporarily forgetting her fears about the wild cat. Kate found her picture almost at once: a crouching wild cat, silhouetted against dark trees, his paws tightly clasping the rock which supported him.

"He's not as beautiful as my cat, but he is, very nearly," Kate said.

Sheina, hunting along the shelves, among china models of dogs and cats and wild animals, found two model cats, made of slate. A black cat, sitting erect, paws neatly together, and a copy of an Egyptian temple cat.

"These are my birthday presents to you," she said, and was rewarded by the flare of pleasure in the child's dark eyes.

As they left the shop Kate saw a model eagle in the window. The bird stood, imperious, wings folded, and sunlight shone on the burnished feathers.

"Have we any money left?" Kate asked. They seemed to have spent a fortune.

"We only spent about half the amount your father gave us," Sheina said. "Why?"

"Dad had a birthday too. I tried to make it special and cooked his favourite supper; it wasn't very nice. I couldn't buy him a present. I hadn't any money. Could I buy him that eagle?"

The bird was expensive, but Sheina thought it would be money well spent. Her present wrapped, Kate went out to the car. The brief elation had gone and only worry remained. She sat like a small ghost of herself on the journey back, wishing the miles away, and then not wishing to arrive.

Suppose the cat wasn't there? Suppose he had died in the night? Suppose a dog had wandered up the hill and killed him; or a fox. He wasn't strong enough to fight. She imagined him lying stiff, nobody near him, never to move again.

Sheina felt as if she had a different child beside her. A handsome child. Kate was no beauty but she had a strong face, and later would be a very striking-looking woman. The neat cap of hair suited her. She was slim and graceful and the new clothes accentuated that.

But the haunted eyes still stared out of the white face and it would take a long time to heal the traumas of the past year. She could not even reassure the child. She felt it most unlikely that the cat would still be in the cave, and not have left it during the night for an easier hunting ground. It was unfair to raise false hopes.

The sun had gone by the time they reached the hills. Clouds hid the sky. Soon it would rain.

Kate stood by the car, looking up the hill towards the cave.

Was he there?

Or had he died in the night, or limped far from the hill, away from the scent of the dog, before they found time to set the cage? Her pleasure in the day was dimming, her worry again uppermost in her mind. The wild cat was hers, in a way that nobody else would ever understand. And she might fail him.

Sheina watched Kate climb. Minutes stretched into eternity as the tiny figure plodded up among the teasing heather clumps that threatened to trip her. Kate looked back once, and then climbed on. It was steep and she was exhausted, not yet recovered from the night spent on the moors.

She shivered, but not from cold. Please God, let him be there. Please listen. Did God listen? Was there a God, or only a cruel Power that gloried in pain?

The cave was a dark shadow against the grey rock. She paused, listening for a sound, but there was no sound except the faint drip drip of water somewhere inside. She remembered how a tiny spring had wetted the walls beside the crack and once the cat had drunk from the little pool that formed.

She reached the darkness. It was difficult to see inside.

And then she reached the cage. She knew, as soon as she touched the top of it, that the door had fallen into place and he must be trapped.

He was crouching inside his prison. He had been lying in the dark, afraid, and cold. The smell of the dog lingered. There had been warmth against the girl who had slept in the outer cave, and suddenly her smell was there, and his memory was triggered. If he could get to her he would be warm again. As he crept towards the opening of his hiding place, the heady smell of new-killed rabbit came to him. He gave way to the rage of hunger and tore at the life-giving flesh. Little remained but the bones.

Kate dragged the cage out and looked at him. His fur stared, the gleam of health gone. The great eyes were dull. He had little energy. He did not even raise his head. Only the slight movement of an ear showed that he was aware of her presence.

Kate waved. Sheina left the car and climbed the hill. She looked down at the cat, who made only a token hiss.

The injury was worse than she had thought. He could never survive.

Kate sat in the back seat of the car, the cage balanced beside her. The cat lay still, too weak to protest, although he hated the smell of this strange place and its uncanny movement. Once or twice he hissed softly. The girl was beside him, her scent overwhelming him, and he trusted her.

Ruaraidh whistled when he saw the wound.

"I'll do all I can," he promised. "He'll have to stay here tonight, and maybe longer. You can't have him free around the place when he comes back to you. He'll need nursing; and he may be very difficult to handle. He's a true wild cat, not a tame cat gone wild. They take a lot of taming. I've never known one really tamed."

Ruaraidh did not know that his mother had been a domestic cat. "He'll need a safe cage. You won't be able to touch him or trust him."

Kate, looking at the torn shoulder, was afraid. The vet, watching her, newly clothed, her hair neatly cut, was surprised by the child's appearance. She had looked such an Orphan Annie before, a waif, uncared for.

He smiled at her.

"I've mended worse than this," he said,

his fingers crossed behind him. He did not want to upset her now. She had had enough to take in the past two days. He had been among the searchers on the hill and Sheina had told him the child's story. Let her get used to the idea of the inevitable loss slowly. It was a very odd alliance, a lonely child and a solitary wild beast. "There's always hope. He's a strong animal, to have lasted so long. He's eaten and so is still trying to survive. Ring me in the morning."

Kate helped Sheina prepare the evening meal. The girl was used to cooking, but had never made a curry, and was intrigued by the process.

Kate drained the rice and served it on to the plates. Gavin's Land-Rover had just drawn up at the door.

"I've been thinking," Sheina said, as they waited for him to walk up the path. Kate looked at her expectantly.

"You can come with me to school. I'll drop you off at the back gate so that nobody sees us; and pick you up there. A secret. OK?"

"OK."

Gavin, ducking his head as he entered,

was startled to be greeted by an excited daughter eager to show him her new picture, and the two model cats. She looked a different child, and only now did he realise how uncared for she had been. Her new clothes had given her confidence. The knowledge that he hadn't forgotten her birthday after all, and that he had allowed her to choose so much, and to buy the picture for her room, seemed to heal the breach between them. She bubbled over, talking as if the years had held speech behind a dam that had now burst.

"I've got a birthday present for you," she said. She watched anxiously as he took the small parcel. Her eyes never left his face as he opened it and Sheina held her breath, praying that he wouldn't say the wrong thing, that he would like it, and even if he didn't would appreciate the thought behind the choice.

"He's magnificent," Gavin said, as the light glinted on the bronze feathers. The bird, placed on the table, stared back at him out of amber-coloured eyes.

He bent to kiss his daughter, and she

hugged him tight, needing his caress. He held her as if he would never let go, and Sheina, watching, felt a sudden stir of her own emotions and the unwelcome knowledge that it would take very little for this man and his child to hold a major place in her own affections. Perhaps even . . .

She brushed away her thoughts. She had vowed never to be vulnerable again. It was a relief to turn to mundane matters and dish the curry.

Sheina's cottage was warm, bright with colour. The walls were hung with photographs, enlarged, of the local lochs. Trees in winter, in high summer, and autumn coloured, brilliant with light that seemed to glow within each landscape. Gavin, when he had eaten, stared at them.

"Your work?" he asked.

She nodded, and suddenly they were plunged into a technical discussion, as he realised that Sheina knew a good deal of his craft.

"Can I show you my film? See what you think? I could do with help with editing, with a second opinion."

He had come to life, and Sheina, watching him, was startled by the light in the eyes so like Kate's, and the sudden ease with which he talked, as if she were a colleague, sharing his work, understanding his work. As indeed, she discovered as he talked, she did.

"We could all get in the hide," he said. "I doubt if it would disturb the birds. They're used to my scent. If you put my anoraks on over your own . . ."

Sheina was worried about her new responsibilities. She drove over very early, and watched Kate, wearing one of her new outfits, gobble her breakfast, edgy with impatience to find out how the cat was faring.

Sunday was often a dreary day for all of them. Today was highlighted.

First of all there was the phone call to Ruaraidh.

The cat had been operated on, he said. The operation was a success but the animal was very weak indeed. He was on a drip and would have to stay on for a couple of days. Until then, it was impossible to say whether he would live. There had been a great deal of infection, and he might have blood poisoning.

Kate had made up her mind. The cat was going to live. She would nurse him back to full strength. It had to happen. She asked if they could go to church and while there she prayed as she had never prayed before, asking for the wild cat's life in return for her own good behaviour for ever.

Sheina was determined to salvage pleasure from the day. She and Kate would work in the cottage garden and try to restore it. It would make such a difference to the place. Next summer would see it bright with old-time flowers. She had a vivid vision of the old vet approving of her enthusiasm.

Kate worked hard, inspired by Sheina. They weeded until their hands were sore and then sat in the sun to eat sandwiches made from grated cheese and pickle which Kate thought the best she had ever tasted.

They spent the afternoon improving the cottage. Sheina had a blue and white rug that she did not need, and it brightened Kate's little room. There were hooks for a curtain across the rail, and Sheina draped these with a sheet of brilliant blue.

She hung the cat picture. The wild cat stared at them with inscrutable eyes.

Kate put her two model cats on the mantelpiece.

She looked at the picture. If only her cat would live. He must live. He must.

Kate and Sheina inspected the shed at the bottom of the cottage garden. It needed cleaning out and they set to work, spending the rest of the day scrubbing the floor and walls.

"I think we might borrow a cage from my keeper friend," Sheina said, as they worked. Kate, feeling that she was helping her cat, laughed and chattered, suddenly a different child.

"It all looks so different," she said as she laid the table for supper. Sheina had brought over a bright checked scarlet and white tablecloth. The cloths in the cottage were yellow check and Kate hated them.

There was an air of festivity. Kate added a bowl of wild daisies. She felt as if it were a party.

They had just finished eating when

there was a knock on the front door.

"Visitors?" Sheina said. "I never have visitors on a Sunday. Aren't you lucky?"

Kate, opening the door, stared up at the postman. He was unfamiliar in his Sunday clothes and beside him was one of the boys in her class, a red-headed lad named Grant McLeod.

"Grant is my grandson," the postman said. "The children were worried about you; we wanted to see how you are. None the worse for your adventure?"

Grant was staring at Kate. This was not the girl he knew at school in her weird clothes with hair that looked as if it had been hacked about by a pair of blunt scissors. She was completely different, looking like a model out of a magazine and not the Kate they had teased for being so odd.

He held out a small parcel.

"Ma mother made some scones for ye," he said. "She thought maybe you and your father didn't bake ever. A wee lassie and a man."

Sheina grinned at the postman who looked startled by his grandson's frankness.

"We never do bake," Kate said. "That's

lovely. My father adores scones. My mother used to make them and we had them hot with jam and cream like they do in Cornwall. Come in for a coffee," she suggested, and the postman walked inside, and put his cap down on the oak chest by the front door. After a moment Grant followed them.

The children sat in silence, neither knowing what to say, Grant somewhat overawed by the girl who seemed now to be a total stranger. He had never known her well. His grandfather, talking to him, had discovered how the children had tormented Kate at school and thought that this probably accounted in part for her running away. Grant had had a long lecture on unkindness, and was feeling shame.

He did not know how to make amends, and Kate did not know what to say to him. She was thankful when the pair took their leave.

"There's a box on the doorstep," Gavin said, staring down.

The box had Kate's name on it.

Sheina lifted it and took it inside.

"For me?" Kate was disbelieving. Too

much was happening, all at once.

The box was filled with tiny parcels. Each one bore her name and that of one of the children in her form. A book; a bar of chocolate; a tiny model of a horse; a pencil. From Morag and Rita and Laura and Jean; from Hamish and Duncan and Donald and Sandy.

They took them up the stairs to Kate's room. She put them on the window sill: tiny ornaments; a little picture of a girl and a dog; pencils and notebooks and several books to read and enough sweets to last her a month.

Later that evening Hector, the policeman, came by, also bringing a gift, of a carved wooden seal which he had made himself. With him came the news that he had a new little son. "You must come and see him," he said.

Kate went back to school in a happier mood. The children were wary, and not welcoming, but nobody teased her. They stared at her new clothes and one of the girls asked her to join in a game of ball at break. Sheina, watching, felt relief. It would take time, but it was a beginning.

The week dragged by. The cat was not eating. Ruaraidh, watching him, thought he would probably die before Saturday came. Kate, her mind focused on the cat throughout the week, was unable to concentrate. Her schoolwork suffered even more. Ruaraidh would not even let her see him, saying it might upset him. Not saying that it would upset her.

He was a wild beast caged, and might not accept captivity at all. He might prefer to die.

12

BY the middle of the second week there was a change. The wound was healing. The wild cat had accepted help, apathetically. He was too weak to struggle. Too weak to care. Too weak to resent his surroundings. His days were compounded of alien smells and of pain.

When he slept he dreamed of the wild moors and the heather tang; of roaming on the beaches, the tide far out, and the pools full of little fish that flapped and struggled as he angled for them. He dreamed of full moon nights and the scents of the hills.

He dreamed of hunting and twitched as he dreamed.

He dreamed of hunger; an aching hunger that dominated every other feeling. He woke ravenous. Ruaraidh gave him half a new-killed rabbit, the fur still on the body, and watched him tear it. Memory was triggered, of the long stalk, the pounce, the kill, and the warm flesh that satisfied his needs. He crouched, swearing softly as he ate, and the man watching left the cat in peace to savour his meal.

He knew as he closed the door behind him, that this cat would never settle in a human home. He was totally wild, a creature born to hunt and kill, to run free under the stars and live out his life on the moors and the steep slopes of the high hills.

Ruaraidh rang early on the Friday morning to say that Kate could visit and that if all went well she could take the cat home and keep him until he was fit again. But then he must go free.

Kate thought the day would never end. The clock ticked remorselessly, so slowly. Every minute lasted an hour. Every lesson was an eternity to be endured until at last she was released to meet Sheina, and be driven over to look at her protegé.

He was in a large cage in a stable behind the vet's house, on his own. Ruaraidh did not think the cat would ever settle in a room where there were dogs, as well as other cats, recovering from surgery. Kate hoped that he would know her, but he gave no sign that she was any different to anyone else.

She crouched and spoke to him, but he lay still, watching her, making no move towards her. Only his moving ears showed that he was aware of her. His eyes were expressionless, his body crouched and rigid. He was not accepting man.

"He's forgotten me," she said. She could not bear the disappointment.

"He's still a very sick cat," Ruaraidh said. "It will be days before he is fit again. He may remember you again when he lives with you, but don't get too fond of him, Kate. He's a wild animal, and will never be really tame. He would suffer terribly kept in a cage and if you keep him like a normal cat, and let him roam, he'll take to the hills as soon as he is well enough and never come back again."

Kate wasn't listening. There was always a first time and she dreamed of the cat becoming her cat, never wanting to leave her, needing her as she needed him. She counted the days to the end of the next week, when Ruaraidh had said she could take him home. She could keep him in the big cage that the vet had borrowed from the zoo. It gave him room to walk a few paces and stretch and stand and turn.

The days at school had to be endured. The other children were less wary of her. She joined in some of their games, though there was still an uneasiness. The Head had lectured them when Kate ran away, telling them how lonely she was and how cruel they had been to her. Sheina had not realised until Kate began to talk to her, just how much the child had suffered from her classmates. Children could be hateful. Far worse than adults at times, never thinking at all of the other person's feelings.

Grant had become her protector. When the cat came home he was the only child in the class allowed to visit, and that very briefly. Sheina and Gavin began to worry, though they did not share their worry. Kate spent the evenings crouched by the cage, talking softly.

She longed to have the animal acknowledge her.

She thought of him when she was at school; she dreamed of him at night. She planned her days around him, living only for the moment when the last lesson bell rang her release, and she could gather her books and fly to meet Sheina and sit, impatient for the journey to end, so that she could see him, could talk to him. She could now safely enter his cage and hand feed him.

She had a name for him in her mind, but it was not a name to be shared. He was Apollo, more beautiful than any other living creature, a god among cats.

Sheina began to think the child was obsessed, beyond all sense or reason. She tried to warn Kate, but words meant nothing. The cat meant everything. He was hers. She had saved his life and surely he would turn to her, would recognise this, would be grateful.

Then, one afternoon, when she had spent the whole of two lessons dreaming and agonising, she took him a chicken leg, as a change from his diet of rabbit.

He received it almost with disbelief, smelling it, licking it, tasting it. For the moment he was all domestic cat, his mother dominant. He stared at Kate, the source of such intense pleasure, and left the food for an instant to rub round her legs, leaving the scent from his cheek glands on her, marking her for his own.

She dared not move or breathe. He was communicating with her, telling her how much he appreciated this savoury treasure. He began to eat, crouching over it, tearing at it, but coming back to her to weave ecstatically against her, even while he was chewing.

Kate was enchanted. She wished she could bring him chicken more often, but it was a rare part of their own diet as her father did not like eating fowl. Sheina had saved the leg for him.

The cat was feeling better, the ache in his shoulder almost a memory, the skin healed and the fur beginning to grow. Walking was painful and he limped badly on one front leg. He practised taking the weight on it daily, and lay down as soon as it hurt. He could stand for longer periods now.

Kate, watching him, was fascinated. He stretched, and began to pace, a few steps this way, a few that, gradually taking more and more weight on the injured side. One step, lie down and rest. Two steps, lie down and rest.

At times he sat and washed himself, his tongue rasping over his fur, or sat, back leg in the air over one shoulder, cleaning himself underneath. It was hard to believe he was wild. He was so like a domestic cat in every way.

Except for the sudden hiss when she moved unwarily, or when she brought a stranger to see him. Then his fur was fluffed so that he was a giant cat, and his eyes glared, and the hissing changed to a slow warning swear.

One day he would change. One day he would learn that those Kate brought to see him meant no harm. One day he would be hers, entirely.

Kate thought of all this as she brought him his food. She had not given him chicken again, but reverted to his diet of rabbit. Gavin reminded her that there were free range chickens all round them; suppose he changed his diet? There would be guns raised against him in earnest then.

"Dad, it's cooked chicken," Kate said patiently, wondering why adults were always so obtuse. "It smells quite different to live chicken." But she did heed him.

Kate was beyond her father's reach and beyond Sheina's. She was going to keep her cat with her, and whether he wanted chicken or not didn't matter. He wouldn't leave her side. He would follow her, doglike. She would provide his food. He would never be hungry, or need to hunt again. She shut her mind to reason.

He smelled the rabbit leg and came to the mesh. Kate held it in her hand, and pushed it through, and he took it from her fingers. He looked at her, and quite suddenly gave a soft mew, and then began to purr as he crouched to eat.

For the next few days he took food from her, and then, one Sunday morning, as he leaned against the bars, he purred, loud and long, and rubbed against the wire, and when she put her hand against it, rubbed against that.

He was hers. He was safe. He would never leave her, even if they did let him go free. He would be back, wanting her, needing her. They were all wrong. She sat, listening to the throaty purr, loving the cat beyond any creature she had ever known, longing to open the cage and take him and nurse him.

It was a rusty disused purr, as if he had forgotten the skill. Kate held her breath, listening.

There was a shine on his coat again. There was light in the great eyes that watched her, and though he still fluffed his fur and spat when Gavin or Sheina came by, he no longer spat at Kate.

Sheina, passing, looked in. Gavin and Kate had become important to her, filling a gap in her own life that she had not realised existed. She made more and more excuses to pass the cottage and make sure that all was well. Aware too of the deficiencies in catering, as neither Gavin nor Kate was an expert cook, she began to come over each evening and share their evening meal, cooking it for them, adding inspired treats. She was more and more welcome, not only for the pleasure that her cooking gave them, but also for herself.

Kate loved talking to her, and the evenings when her father was late were no longer lonely. Gavin found Sheina's adult presence more than welcome when he came in tired, and her company was soothing. Soon the three of them were looking together at the filming, discussing the eagles and their behaviour, savouring the sight of the great birds soaring over the crags and the greedy youngster begging for food.

Now, as she passed, she saw the child's rapt face, and heard the unusual sound and identified it. She wished it hadn't happened. It would make things infinitely worse.

"Oh, Kate, Kate," she thought, but she knew that nothing she said had any effect.

Gavin spent his days filming. The young eagle was fledged and soon would start his first attempts at flight. But somehow worry about Kate intruded even during the day, and focused at night when he lay watching the night-time sky and the bright remote stars, and wished that his wife was still alive. He had no idea how to help his daughter.

When talking with Sheina about his work he sometimes raised the subject of Kate, knowing she was living in a dream world, and that soon it must be shattered.

The cat could never live his life in a cage. One day, he must be freed. It was far from easy to care for him, and he spat furiously at everyone but Kate.

As soon as she had eaten she ran outside, spending the evening sitting by the cage, refusing to come in until it was too dark to see. She was sure there was communication between them; that the cat was beginning to love her, and that one day he would be hers completely, roaming perhaps by day but coming back to her each night, looking for companionship.

Ruaraidh, coming to look at his patient, was equally worried. Kate stood politely in front of him, listening, but he knew she did not believe a word he said. She had closed her mind to all of them. He had teenagers of his own.

"You can help them, do your best for them, but that's all," he said one evening to Sheina and Gavin, joining them over coffee, leaving Kate crouching, her eyes rapt, as she talked to her protegé. "They go their own way; maybe find a path to hell for themselves and all we can do is suffer as we watch them burn. They'll never believe we care."

Sheina, startled at the sudden bitterness in his voice, wondered what had prompted the comment, but did not ask. Ruaraidh's elder son was nineteen and living away from home and even at school he had been a wild lad. Not much harm in him, but he took crazy risks and never saw danger and believed everything he was told.

"Kate was always a dreamer," Gavin said. "A romantic. She loves the old legends, of Arthur and the Round Table; of Cuchulain and the Hound of Ulster. She always wanted a dog like that; dedicated to her, giving his life for her, totally devoted."

Sheina, clearing away the dishes as Gavin and Ruaraidh sat and watched the day's film sequence, shivered. It was a recipe for disaster. Kate was lost in a world they could not share.

Spilling washing-up liquid into the bowl, she had a sudden vision of herself, aged ten, small, angry, raging at her father who was selling her pony in order to buy another that was big enough for her. It had seemed like selling a member of the family, a total treachery, and for weeks she had been inconsolable and refused even to look at the pretty little mare that occupied her first love's stable. She had never let herself love the second pony so much.

"You can't live their lives for them. They have to learn for themselves," she said, returning to the living room, and both men stared at her, having forgotten the earlier topic of conversation.

★ ★ ★

Night after night the cat, watching the moon ride up the sky, dreamed of the high hills and longed for freedom. He tried to break the mesh with claws and teeth, but the cage was strong, and he could not free himself.

Kate watched the same moon and thought of him. Apollo, Lord of the Moors, tamed and obedient to her will, with the other children envying and admiring. Kate, who could tame wild animals. Orpheus with his lute had charmed the beasts so that they followed

227

him. Seals came to music. Maybe if she sang to her cat . . .

The days passed by. The trees were summer weary, autumn a moonspan away. The cat yearned for the hills.

Whenever they spoke of freeing him, Kate stopped listening. An obstinate expression came on to her face, and they knew that she hoped against all reason that this cat would become hers, and stay with them throughout his life.

There were times when Gavin was jealous of the cat. Sheina, watching him, knew that she had broken her own rules, had become involved, and what was worse, was once more vulnerable. If Gavin and his daughter went away she would feel as Kate was going to feel when the cat was freed.

Totally bereft.

Ruaraidh came to look at his patient twelve weeks after they had caught him.

"Time for your warrior to go," Ruaraidh said. "He's well, Kate, and he's pining for freedom. We can't keep him. It's cruel."

Kate said nothing. The cat was hers and he would stay with her for life.

228

"Come with me, Kate," Ruaraidh said. He led her to the bottom of the garden and leaned against the rough stone wall.

It was twilight, and a giant red sun was dying over the loch.

"Look. Out there is the water, the sea that comes and goes daily, leaving little pools on the tide. There your cat fished. He was free to come, and free to go. And up there on the hills he could run under the night sky; could hunt and feed, could sleep under the bright stars. He knew freedom, Kate."

Kate's dark eyes were looking up at him, and this time, he thought, she was listening.

"Suppose I took you and caged you; or shut you day and night in a dark room, never to come out. No room to run, or jump. No wind on your face, no grass under your feet; only the bars, and the little window that shows the light by day and the stars by night, and reminds you of long ago when you were able to go where you wished and do as you wished. Only the stink of the cage; your own stink, even though it is cleaned out; only the

229

food they give you, that someone else caught."

Sheina and Gavin watched from the window, wondering what the vet was saying to the child. The two were outlined against the sky, almost motionless. Ruaraidh took Kate by the shoulders and turned her to face the hills.

"There he could run and he could jump; he knew freedom and exultation; he knew the long stalk and the thrill of the kill and the satisfaction of eating. He knew ecstasy and excitement. And now he lives his days in semi-darkness, trapped. No more racing on the windy beach; no more darting his paw into the little pools; no more running through the dew-wet heather, reading the news on the wind. Only four wooden walls and the bars until he dies, Kate. Are you going to condemn him to life imprisonment?"

He walked away, leaving her.

"I feel like a traitor," he said, as he went indoors.

"Look," Gavin said. He had thought of half a solution, in the long night hours when he questioned everything in the world. It might help; it was worth a try. "Can you find her a kitten? Tabby, if possible; not one that's fluffy and appealing. Preferably one that nobody wants, or has been rescued from somewhere? One that will appeal to her sympathy; she won't take to one that's been bred as a pet. It must be in need of help; maybe of nursing."

"That won't be difficult," Ruaraidh said. "I know just where to get one like that. It will cost you a good bit in vet fees; it can be brought back to health, but it will need a lot of care. There's a litter I've been given; the cat was a stray and she had them in the wild, and was run over. One of the shepherds found the kits and brought them in. They were still blind when I got them and we've been hand rearing them. They're pathetic little things, but they'll survive, in the end, given TLC."

"TLC?" Gavin was startled.

Sheina and Ruaraidh laughed.

"Tender loving care," Sheina said. It was something she wanted to offer herself to these two humans who had somehow been tossed like flotsam into her life.

That night Kate came in long after

dark and went, white faced and silent, to her room, saying nothing to either of them. She lay awake for a long time, needing to cry, but she was grown up now and tears were for babies.

She heard a vixen bark softly and her cubs answered. Far away an engine revved as it took the hill and then dropped away into silence. An owl called. Soft and low and mysterious, a sound that the cat heard, and lifted his head, and answered. She heard his long-drawn wail. He had never cried like that before.

The wind grew and flung the waves against the beach and she knew the cat was listening. That he would be awake, looking out of the little window that gave him his only glimpse of the wide world that had once been his. Listening to the rush of the wind and maybe dreaming of days when he had been free.

Free to run and to jump. Free to climb the steeps, and free to run the beaches. Free to hunt. He was a wild creature still, and he would remain wild all his life. Although he accepted her, his own world still called him. She had no right to imprison him for her own benefit.

She could remember him, and she did not want to remember him caged and shabby, all the bright life dimmed in him, as he suffered and longed to be released.

He had to go.

And he had to go now or she could not bear it.

She dressed, quietly, and went out to the shed. She opened the cage. She watched the cat. He came out and looked at her doubtfully. She went down the path and through the gate and he followed her. Once he brushed against her, as she led him along the night-dark path that bordered the edge of the loch. Along the road away from the cottage, her footsteps soft on the ground, and the pad pad pad of the cat behind her as if he knew where she was leading him.

There was a bright moon that silvered the water and shone on the bracken and heather. The far out tide foamed white at the edge of glistening sands, and there was a band of light in the loch, a shimmer that moved and drifted, as if a moonstruck giant had painted the waves with phosphorescence.

There was nothing in the world but her and the cat.

She came to the edge of the hill where they had sheltered in the cave, and turned and knelt. The cat came to her, and rubbed against her, purring, as if thanking her for his liberty, and perhaps for her care of him.

And then he was gone, fleetfoot, up among the rocks, leaping and jumping, once turning his head and opening his mouth in a raucous mew that echoed in the night and seemed to say goodbye to her for ever.

She watched him go. He was fast and fit and his coat gleamed, and he had followed her and rubbed against her, and then he had left her.

She crouched for a long time, watching the hillside, longing for another glimpse of him, but it was as if he had never existed.

Slowly she went back, glad of the darkness. She closed the door on the empty cage, and closed the door of the silent shed, and slipped into the house just as the first cocks began to crow on the distant farm.

She washed, and cooked the breakfast.

Gavin, smelling bacon, came downstairs.

"I let him go," she said. "Last night," and couldn't say any more because the tears threatened to spill over. It was weeks before she was able to tell Sheina and her father exactly what she had done. They could only guess.

Kate walked round white faced, lost in her misery. Neither could help her. No one could help her. The evenings were light and Gavin bought her a bicycle. She cycled over to the hill, day after day, but there was no sign of the cat anywhere. Once she found part of a rabbit, half eaten, and thought that maybe he was there, but it could have been a fox.

She had to learn to live with loss. Why did it have to happen? Why had God taken her mother? Why couldn't he let the cat visit her, need her, want her? There were never any answers.

Late one evening there was a ring at the door.

Kate went to answer it. Sheina and her father were engrossed.

Ruaraidh stood there, looking down at her.

"I've a favour to ask. I need your help," he said, ducking his head as her father did as he went through the low door into the living room. He held out a small bag, its zip half open.

Kate took it. She stared.

There, on a white towel, lay a tiny tabby kitten, staring up at her with green eyes. It was starvation thin, and so frail that she wondered if it were dying.

"He needs a home. The shepherd found him and his two sisters. He was born in the wild and his mother, who was a domestic cat gone astray, was killed by a car. We've been hand rearing them, but now they're due to be weaned it's taking so much time. He's going to be a fit cat one day. But only if someone takes a great deal of trouble with him. You can bring him to me at first while you are at school and one of my nurses will feed him during the day. It isn't far out of Sheina's way. It will only be for a couple of weeks, and then maybe your father can slip home at lunchtime and give him his midday feed. He'll need tiny meals, just a teaspoonful of a special mix I'll give you, every two hours, until he begins to digest properly. They've had a lot of problems, these mites. I know I can trust you."

Kate lifted the kitten and held it close against her. It wasn't the same as her beautiful Apollo, but it was hers for ever. Her very own cat.

"What are you going to call him?" Ruaraidh held out a finger and the kitten patted at it.

Kate looked out at the hill beyond the window, at the long stretch of blue loch and the tangled weed. The tangle had healed her, and her father. She turned to look at Sheina, but the woman was absorbed, and Ruaraidh, following the child's eyes, nodded his head as if a question had been asked and answered.

They went out into the shadowy garden. The sun was dying in a riot of red, and black clouds flew across the sky. Something moved in the bushes, and Kate held her breath, as the wild cat came towards her, on soft paws that made no sound.

Ruaraidh, behind her, did not move.

The cat came towards the girl, rubbed briefly round her legs, as if caressing her, purring throatily. He dropped something at her feet, looked up at her, and mewed. Then he was off, speeding over the wall.

Kate looked down at the dead rabbit she had just been given, and then watched the ripple in the undergrowth where the swift body moved.

She held the kitten closer against her body, feeling the tiny throb as it purred.

"I'm going to call him Warrior," she said. "I hope he'll be as brave as my wild cat, and fight his way through to health."

The sun flared and died and darkness shadowed the garden. That night, lying in her bed, the kitten tucked against her, Kate heard movements outside her window, and knew that though the wild cat had found freedom, he had not forgotten her.

Nor would she, as long as she lived, forget him.

TO FIGHT THE WILD
Rod Ansell and Rachel Percy

Lost in uncharted Australian bush, Rod Ansell survived by hunting and trapping wild animals, improvising shelter and using all the bushman's skills he knew.

COROMANDEL
Pat Barr

India in the 1830s is a hot, uncomfortable place, where the East India Company still rules. Amelia and her new husband find themselves caught up in the animosities which seethe between the old order and the new.

THE SMALL PARTY
Lillian Beckwith

A frightening journey to safety begins for Ruth and her small party as their island is caught up in the dangers of armed insurrection.

FATAL RING OF LIGHT
Helen Eastwood

Katy's brother was supposed to have died in 1897 but a scrawled note in his handwriting showed July 1899. What had happened to him in those two years? Katy was determined to help him.

NIGHT ACTION
Alan Evans

Captain David Brent sails at dead of night to the German occupied Normandy town of St. Jean on a mission which will stretch loyalty and ingenuity to its limits, and beyond.

A MURDER TOO MANY
Elizabeth Ferrars

Many, including the murdered man's widow, believed the wrong man had been convicted. The further murder of a key witness in the earlier case convinced Basnett that the seemingly unrelated deaths were linked.

THE WILDERNESS WALK
Sheila Bishop

Stifling unpleasant memories of a misbegotten romance in Cleave with Lord Francis Aubrey, Lavinia goes on holiday there with her sister. The two women are thrust into a romantic intrigue involving none other than Lord Francis.

THE RELUCTANT GUEST
Rosalind Brett

Ann Calvert went to spend a month on a South African farm with Theo Borland and his sister. They both proved to be different from her first idea of them, and there was Storr Peterson — the most disturbing man she had ever met.

ONE ENCHANTED SUMMER
Anne Tedlock Brooks

A tale of mystery and romance and a girl who found both during one enchanted summer.

CLOUD OVER MALVERTON
Nancy Buckingham

Dulcie soon realises that something is seriously wrong at Malverton, and when violence strikes she is horrified to find herself under suspicion of murder.

AFTER THOUGHTS
Max Bygraves

The Cockney entertainer tells stories of his East End childhood, of his RAF days, and his post-war showbusiness successes and friendships with fellow comedians.

MOONLIGHT
AND MARCH ROSES
D. Y. Cameron

Lynn's search to trace a missing girl takes her to Spain, where she meets Clive Hendon. While untangling the situation, she untangles her emotions and decides on her own future.

NURSE ALICE IN LOVE
Theresa Charles

Accepting the post of nurse to little Fernie Sherrod, Alice Everton could not guess at the romance, suspense and danger which lay ahead at the Sherrod's isolated estate.

POIROT INVESTIGATES
Agatha Christie

Two things bind these eleven stories together — the brilliance and uncanny skill of the diminutive Belgian detective, and the stupidity of his Watson-like partner, Captain Hastings.

LET LOOSE THE TIGERS
Josephine Cox

Queenie promised to find the long-lost son of the frail, elderly murderess, Hannah Jason. But her enquiries threatened to unlock the cage where crucial secrets had long been held captive.

THE TWILIGHT MAN
Frank Gruber

Jim Rand lives alone in the California desert awaiting death. Into his hermit existence comes a teenage girl who blows both his past and his brief future wide open.

DOG IN THE DARK
Gerald Hammond

Jim Cunningham breeds and trains gun dogs, and his antagonism towards the devotees of show spaniels earns him many enemies. So when one of them is found murdered, the police are on his doorstep within hours.

THE RED KNIGHT
Geoffrey Moxon

When he finds himself a pawn on the chessboard of international espionage with his family in constant danger, Guy Trent becomes embroiled in moves and countermoves which may mean life or death for Western scientists.

TIGER TIGER
Frank Ryan

A young man involved in drugs is found murdered. This is the first event which will draw Detective Inspector Sandy Woodings into a whirlpool of murder and deceit.

CAROLINE MINUSCULE
Andrew Taylor

Caroline Minuscule, a medieval script, is the first clue to the whereabouts of a cache of diamonds. The search becomes a deadly kind of fairy story in which several murders have an other-worldly quality.

LONG CHAIN OF DEATH
Sarah Wolf

During the Second World War four American teenagers from the same town join the Army together. Forty-two years later, the son of one of the soldiers realises that someone is systematically wiping out the families of the four men.

THE LISTERDALE MYSTERY
Agatha Christie

Twelve short stories ranging from the light-hearted to the macabre, diverse mysteries ingeniously and plausibly contrived and convincingly unravelled.

TO BE LOVED
Lynne Collins

Andrew married the woman he had always loved despite the knowledge that Sarah married him for reasons of her own. So much heartache could have been avoided if only he had known how vital it was to be loved.

ACCUSED NURSE
Jane Converse

Paula found herself accused of a crime which could cost her her job, her nurse's reputation, and even the man she loved, unless the truth came to light.

BUTTERFLY MONTANE
Dorothy Cork

Parma had come to New Guinea to marry Alec Rivers, but she found him completely disinterested and that overbearing Pierce Adams getting entirely the wrong idea about her.

HONOURABLE FRIENDS
Janet Daley

Priscilla Burford is happily married when she meets Junior Environment Minister Alistair Thurston. Inevitably, sexual obsession and political necessity collide.

WANDERING MINSTRELS
Mary Delorme

Stella Wade's career as a concert pianist might have been ruined by the rudeness of a famous conductor, so it seemed to her agent and benefactor. Even Sir Nicholas fails to see the possibilities when John Tallis falls deeply in love with Stella.

CHATEAU OF FLOWERS
Margaret Rome

Alain, Comte de Treville needed a wife to look after him, and Fleur went into marriage on a business basis only, hoping that eventually he would come to trust and care for her.

CRISS-CROSS
Alan Scholefield

As her ex-husband had succeeded in kidnapping their young daughter once, Jane was determined to take her safely back to England. But all too soon Jane is caught up in a new web of intrigue.

DEAD BY MORNING
Dorothy Simpson

Leo Martindale's body was discovered outside the gates of his ancestral home. Is it, as Inspector Thanet begins to suspect, murder?